Jason *and* Marceline

Other Books Available in Paperback by Jerry Spinelli:

Maniac Magee

Space Station Seventh Grade

Who Put That Hair in My Toothbrush?

Jason *and* Marceline

Jerry Spinelli

Little, Brown and Company
Boston   New York   London

First Paperback Edition

Library of Congress Cataloging-in-Publication Data
Spinelli, Jerry.
    Jason and Marceline.

    Summary: The further adventures of Jason Herkimer as he tries to cope with the three important things in his life: his relationship with Marceline McAllister, his peer group, and his burgeoning sexuality. Sequel to "Space Station Seventh Grade."
ISBN 0-316-80662-5 (pb)

    [1. Interpersonal relations — Fiction.   2. Schools — Fiction]   I. Title.
PZ7.S75663Jas   1986   [Fic]   86-10622

10 9 8 7 6 5 4 3

COM-MO

Printed in the United States of America

Lana

Jason *and* Marceline

Laughs

As the bus went roaring past, three middle fingers popped up in front of three faces grinning out of the back window.

"See?" I said.

"See what?" said Marceline.

"They're laughing at us."

"Not to mention giving us the finger."

"That's right. Great way to start off ninth grade. Laughed at and fingered in the first five minutes."

She pulled out her sunglasses, shook open the arms. "You could be on that bus. Laughing at me." She slid the shades on.

"No," I said, "I wouldn't. And you know why?" She stared straight ahead. "You wanna know why?" Her head swiveled slow and looked down on me — down more than usual, because the sidewalk sloped toward the street, and she was on the high side. The shades owled at me. She didn't speak. "Because," I said, "it wouldn't bother you."

Her head swiveled away. "Should it?"

"Yeah, it should, yeah. When people laugh at you, it's *supposed* to bother you. If I was on that bus,

I'd laugh at me too. Who walks to school when they live far enough away to take the bus? It's crazy. I deserve to be laughed at, and it bothers me, yeah. I'm not the one that's unusual. You are."

"Guess I'm just a freak of nature."

Another bus went by. More laughing faces. I wished she would take the shades off.

"Marceline —" I held my arm out, stopping her — "tell the truth. If a whole busload of kids came along, and the bus stopped, right here — *right* here — and everybody on the bus — *everybody* — crowded at the windows and started laughing their asses off and pointing and all — at *you* — you mean to tell me that wouldn't bother you?"

She pushed my arm out of the way with her trombone case and moved on. I took this chance to slip around to the high side of her; now my eyes were almost even with hers. I nudged her. "Huh? Tell me it wouldn't."

She sighed. "Jason, why do you keep trying to make me into something I'm not? So Richie Bell will approve of me?"

"Stop changing the subject."

"That *is* the subject. You trying to change me. You wish I were shorter. You wish I didn't play the trombone. You wish I wouldn't wear sunglasses, especially on the way to school. You wish I would ride the bus. If I have so many faults, what are you doing here with me?"

Good question. Since the end of the summer before eighth grade — thirteen months ago — Marceline McAllister and I have been . . . I don't know . . . *something*. I mean, we're more than just friends. I think. I'm sure. On my side, anyway. Like, we talk a lot and ride bikes and do stuff together. She was inside my house (once). I was inside hers (about ten times, mostly in the kitchen; that's where we play Scrabble). I hold doors open for her sometimes — just because I feel like it — and sometimes she holds doors open for me. No Christmas presents. But birthday cards. We never kissed. Yet. But I like her better than the two girls I have kissed. So what do you call us? What *are* we?

"You're crazy," I told her. "I never said anything about sunglasses."

She just smirked, the way she does to let me know she knows I'm lying. She's better than my mother at reading my mind.

"Why don't you give me some credit," I said. "I *am* here."

"You wish you weren't."

"That's a lie. How can you say I don't like being with you?"

"You'd rather be alone with me. It makes you nervous to know other people are watching. You're terrified I might do something to embarrass you."

I laughed. "Terrified?"

Then: radio music, horn blaring, shouting.

"Yo, Herkimer!"

"Hey, Herk the Jerk!"

Tires squealing, crunching the curb. It was Vesto and his car. Vesto turned sixteen over the summer — by far the oldest kid at Avon Oaks J.H.S., maybe at any junior high. His car was a big old Buick, with one door all putty and Rust-Oleum, no hubcaps, and the trunk tied shut with a rope. It was beautiful. And jammed with guys — bodies coming out the tailpipe.

A door twanged open. Little Looie Lopezia fell out, like something from an overstuffed locker. He picked himself up and tunneled his way back in. Among the legs and arms and earphones, Richie's face came into view, practically upside down. "C'mon, Herk. Jump in."

Marceline was half a block up the street and moving.

"Nah, ts'okay, no room."

"Yeah there is — look —" Bodies shifting. Grunts. Curses. Squawks. "There — c'mon."

If any space was there, I sure couldn't see it. "Forget it, man. What do I look like, a maggot?"

"Hell with 'im," came Vesto's voice. The car shot off, leaving me with a faceful of gas and howls.

Marceline was now not only up the street, she was on the other side. Just as I caught up with her, she recrossed.

"Hey," I called over, "waddaya *doing?*"

"Freeing you."

"From what?"

"Me."

I stepped down from the curb. She wheeled. "Don't you dare!"

I froze. "Huh?"

"Stay there."

I kind of laughed, stepped back onto the curb. I looked around. I prayed no bus would come along. "What're you talking about?"

She didn't answer. She went on walking.

"Marceline, I'm supposed to be walking you to school."

"I'm not a dog. *You* don't *walk* me anywhere."

"*With* you. I'm supposed to be walking *with* you."

"You are."

This was insane. Wacko. I had to get back over to her, *had* to —

She wheeled again: "No!"

I backed up onto the curb. Was this happening? Was I dreaming? Was I really walking a girl to school on opposite sides of the street?

Suddenly she yelped. "I've got it!" She put her trombone case down, opened it, took out the trombone parts, jammed them together, and started to toot. After a few notes she called: "Jason, remember how this goes, so I can write it down when we get to school." Then she went on tooting. Right there. Shades and all. On the sidewalk. The morning sun flashing on the slide.

I knew exactly what she was doing. Marceline had

been writing a song. "Trombone Troubadour." All summer long she was stuck on the refrain, couldn't get it right.

She stopped and called: "No, that's no good. Forget that. Don't remember it. Now wait —" She tried some new toots. "There — that's better. Start remembering —" she lifted the horn to her lips, took a deep breath — "*now!*"

A bus went by. For three or four seconds you couldn't hear the trombone because of all the hooting and howling. The bus driver even gave a toot on *his* horn.

She stopped ("No — that's wrong too. Forget it.") and started ("Okay, try this. Start remembering — *now!*") again.

"That's it!" I yelled. "We're through! Finished! You don't really wanna do all that crazy stuff! You're just daring people to laugh at you! You're a sado-masochist! You lie awake at night thinking up ways to make me look like an idiot! If you think I'm remembering those notes for you — or even *listening* to that slop — you're crazy!"

She pushed the mouthpiece away and just stared at me. Then I felt something against the back of my legs, and another horn, like a trombone from hell, blasted my heart right out of my chest and sent it end-over-end like a fifty-yard field goal. I turned around. Vesto's car was behind me — *right* behind me — on the sidewalk, the bumper touching the back of my jeans.

Door twang. "This time," Richie grinned, "y'either come with us or you're grass."

I got in. I would have even without the threat. The guys cheered. Richie kept pounding me on the back. We jolted back down to street level, Vesto gunned the engine, and the tires peeled a long, high note — the only note I was going to remember.

So I rode to school in style. Naturally, we got mobbed when we pulled up. Vesto could have run for king. He must have driven ten different groups around the block. People were lining up at the curb like it was the loopy roller coaster at Hershey Park.

The bell rang. Everybody groaned and herded inside.

When I reached the second-floor landing, a bunch of kids were at the window, laughing and pointing.

"What's she *doing?*"

"What a weirdo."

"She's even weirder than last year."

"Marceline McBeanpole."

From my place halfway up the last flight of steps, I looked over their heads and saw her across the street: the only one outside, trombone case on the sidewalk, still trying to get it right. A girl's voice sneered, "It's just for attention, the stuff she does. She thinks she's impressing the teachers."

No, I thought, that's not true. She's not trying to impress anybody. This is just the way she is, that's all. She's just being herself, I thought. But I didn't say anything.

I crept up the stairs. I hoped nobody would notice me. Too late —

"Yo, Herkimer! Lookit your lover girl out there!"

I bopped to the top and through the door, pretending not to hear.

The hallway was all bodies. Moving. Surging. Mooing. I brushed against them, bumped off them, slid through them. Voices called my name, first-day voices I hadn't eard since June. I kept moving. The deeper I plunged into the herd, the lonesomer I felt.

A tap on my shoulder.

"Excuse me."

I turned. It was a little kid. Looking up at me. Seventh-grader.

"I think I'm lost. Can you tell me where Homeroom One-Seventeen is?"

I just eyeballed him for a minute. He was the most ridiculous thing I had ever seen. He was wearing inch-thick glasses, his hair was sticking out in ninety different directions, and one of the points of his shirt collar was aiming practically straight up in the air. Then I saw the belt. It was made of hundreds — maybe thousands — of tiny beads. Red, white, and green beads. The green beads made up the shapes of reindeer, antlers and all. The red beads were the reindeer's noses. A whole herd of Rudolphs.

Second bell rang.

"Downstairs," I said, and took off down the nearest steps. I could hear the runt clomping after me. The kids on the first floor had almost all drained into their rooms. I tore up the hall, almost bowling over a homeroom teacher. I prayed I wasn't too late. I slammed through the end doors, down the steps, slammed the heavy main door open . . .

There she was, coming up the walk, kind of bouncy, trombone case swinging. And a proud little grin on her face that said, *I finally got it.*

I held the door open for her. She might have glanced at me, but I couldn't be sure because of the shades. She kept grinning, holding her head high, the way she does, and as she passed by me I hoped — I knew — we weren't finished after all.

Checkin'

The main thing, the first couple days of school, is checkin'. Like, "Hey man, check that out." And, "Hey man, check *that* out!"

It's a checkin'-out orgy. Most of the people you haven't seen all summer, and every one of them — even the nerdiest nerd — is fascinating the first time around. Most of them have changed at least a little bit. Some haven't changed at all, like they spent the summer sitting in homeroom. And then, sometimes, there's somebody who changed so much you'll never recognize her till somebody tells you who she is.

Girls wouldn't understand this, but boys are born with a kind of measuring device, located somewhere behind the eyes, I guess. It kicks in around ninth grade. It's kind of like an artillery range-finder. Whenever a girl comes toward you, it zeroes in instantly on the gazoobies and practically gives you a hard-copy printout on things like size, shape, floppability. But mostly size.

It's incredible, the accuracy. If a girl's balloons gain a millimeter overnight, your range-finder will pick it up. Let a whole summer go by, your fuses start blowing. Everywhere you look — where there was nothing in June, now there's something, and where there was something, now there's *more*.

So. First morning. Richie and I are heading down the hall, when my range-finder picks up something. Still four or five classrooms away, bobbing into view for just an instant at a time, then disappearing into the crowd. But one thing I know already: we're talking size, we're talking great white sharks.

Richie nudges me. He's tracking them too.

Then they come into full view. Under a pink shirt. Bouncy. Very.

A rattling kind of croak comes up from Richie's throat, and he nudges me so hard I fly against some lockers and drop my books. By the time I get everything back together, she's past.

Our eyes speak to each other: "Who was *that?*"

We search our range-finder memory banks. We come up empty.

"Maybe she's new," I say.

"A transfer," Richie says.

"Maybe from a Catholic school."

"Or France."

We spotted her twice again that day. Still no ID.

"Know what?" said Rich.

"What?"

"Maybe she's not a transfer. Maybe she's just one of them quiet people. It's a big school, y'know."

"Rich," I said, "stop and think. You saw 'em. I saw 'em. Our own two eyes. That girl would have to have classes in the mop closet for us never to notice her before."

He couldn't argue with that. A minute later I figured I had the answer. "Maybe it's the clothes. Maybe she always wore loose-fitting clothes before. Baggy, y'know?"

Richie sneered. "I don't care if she was wearing a tablecloth. Them things send out shock waves when they move."

He was right. The range-finder is like an infrared camera — it can detect through camouflage and stuff. If there's a boob anywhere in a room, the range-finder will lock in on it within five seconds. If the Russians ever sent a lady spy over here disguised as a man, she'd never get past the first ninth-grade guy.

It was still a mystery when we met at The Stairwell next day. The Stairwell is an ancient tradition at Avon Oaks J.H. If you're a guy and you're in the ninth grade, it's the place to be in the morning between first and second bells (unless there's a fight to watch). It didn't take long to find out that other guys were wondering about the mystery girl too.

One of them was Vesto. Except he wasn't wondering, he was flat-out saying: "I don't care who it is, I'm getting me a handfulla them babies."

We called Dugan in on the case. That meant getting him to hooky from Holy Ghost, the Catholic high school, which starts at ninth grade. We told him we needed him to see if she was a Catholic-school transfer, and we promised him that even if she wasn't, the hooky would be worth it just to get a gawk at her.

When Dugan showed up that morning, he had his usual tie on, the one he'd been wearing since seventh grade. It used to be red; now it's black. We told him to take it off, it could get him caught, but he wouldn't. Walking down the hallway, we kept Dugan between us. We nudged him as soon as we spotted her, then we all kept quiet till she passed.

We turned to Dugan. He looked glassy-eyed, almost faint.

"Well?" I said. "*Is* she a transfer?"

"I don't think so."

"Well, what?"

He stopped, turned, looked after her as the mob swallowed her up. "Over at Holy Ghost they say they're bigger over here. I thought those were just rumors."

"That's funny," I said. "We heard they were bigger over there."

Dugan spent the rest of the day at A.O., mostly cruising the hallways. He also went to lunch, two study halls, and a Health class.

After Dugan's fizzle, we figured maybe we were letting our emotions get in the way. What we needed was a cool, calm, scientific opinion. Calvin's. Calvin is going to be a doctor, and if there's one thing he knows, it's the human body.

When we told him about the problem, he just

folded his arms and smirked. You could almost see the white coat slip over him. "You don't know who it is, is that right?"

"That's right," I said.

"Okay — I'm going to ask you a question. One question."

"Shoot."

"Did you look at her face?"

I looked at Rich. "Huh?"

"Her face. Face."

"Yeah, we looked," said Rich.

"How long?"

"Enough to see we don't know her."

Calvin just stared at us for a minute, grinning. Then he said, "Lead on."

Well, ol' Doc Calvin stayed cool, but he couldn't come up with a name. All he could say was, "Something's wrong here."

Then there was a voice behind us: "Jewel Fiorito."

We all stood there with our mouths open as Marceline went strolling by. "It's Jewel Fiorito," she sniffed, and turned into her next class.

Belief

It *was* Jewel Fiorito.

At first we didn't believe it. But then we checked out her face real good, and behind the new glasses and new hairdo and new makeup, we started to see traces of the old Jewel.

Others were seeing it too. Next morning at The Stairwell, that's all you heard: "It's Jewel Fiorito! . . . It's Jewel Fiorito!"

Calvin didn't believe it.

"Nobody changes that much," he said.

"Calvin," I said, "a whole summer. A lot can happen."

"Two-and-a-half months. Seventy-five days. They'd have to grow about a quarter of an inch a day."

"So?" I said. "Don't girls develop faster?"

"That's not development, that's explosion. She's human, not popcorn."

Later I was talking to Rich. "Calvin doesn't believe it's Jewel."

"I can't either. It is hard to believe."

"No," I said, "I mean, he *really* doesn't believe it."

"Well, tellya, my mother believes it."

"Yeah? How's that?"

"She saw her at the mall last week."

"Recognized her?"

He snapped his fingers. "Right off the bat."

"Man. Girls, huh? They can't fool each other."

"I guess. She was like that too."

"Your mom?'"

"Yeah. She said she really ballooned out between eighth and ninth grade."

"That's how she said it? *Ballooned?*"

"Yeah, ballooned."

"I don't believe that mother of yours, man."

"Anyway," Rich went on, "she says it's not all it's cracked up to be, having them that big."

"No? How's that?"

"They droop."

"Droop?"

"Yeah. The bigger they are, the more they droop. And the older you get, the more they droop."

"Is that so bad?"

"Sure. What's good about drooping?"

I was heading for study hall after seventh period that day when somebody snatched my shoulder and almost ripped it off. Richie was tearing up the hall with Looie Lopezia and a bunch of other guys. "C'mon!" he yelled back.

I took off. I caught them by the cafeteria turn. Seventh-graders scattered as we stampeded down the hall. I wondered where we were going. We made a quick turn through the door at the foot of a stairway, and suddenly everybody stopped. I was just going to ask what we were doing, when I looked up and saw Jewel make the turn and come ba-ba-bouncing down the lower flight of stairs.

It was incredible. Like they were on rubber bands. I could have sworn she was going to smack herself in the face. She gave a little wave as she went by. The guys all grinned.

"Hi, Jewel."

"Hi, Jewel."

"Hi, Jewel."

I had seen a miracle.

Next morning, in The Stairwell, Vesto was on the radiator. Standing. Piercing the air with a two-fingered whistle. A chill went through me. I knew what was coming. I wanted to pull him down, but it was too late, way too late. There was dead silence, every face gaping up as he told — and showed — how he finally got "them babies" when he gave Jewel a ride in his car the night before.

I didn't wait for him to finish. I headed for homeroom by myself. Something was messed up. Ruined.

Kickoff

They installed lights at the main football field last year, so now the high school has night games. You can see the lights from all over. Everybody goes. Like moths. Except Calvin. He doesn't like sports.

We went. Me, Richie, Dugan, Peter. We all agreed to sneak in, except Peter. He wanted to pay. He's stubborn like that. So while Peter went to a gate, the rest of us scouted around for the best place to climb the fence. We found it at the end of the field opposite the scoreboard, beyond the goalpost. The nearest gate was over by the visitors' stands. A lot of people were lined up. On the track, between us and the goalpost, about twenty feet away, a man was standing with his hands behind his back, facing the field. He wore a blue suit and cap.

I pointed. "Look. Think it's a guard?"

I never got an answer. Dugan and Richie were already mashing themselves to the fence — which was about twice our height — digging their toes into the chain link spaces, climbing up, one careful foot on the top barbs, pushing off — and back down to earth, inside.

"Come on!" Richie waved, and they took off.

The guard turned around. I backed away, made it look like I was heading along the fence to the gate. I kept sneaking peeks. He kept facing the fence.

Then "The Star-Spangled Banner" started. The guard turned his back to me, stood at attention, and saluted.

My chance!

I reached up, got a good hold, dug my toes in, and started climbing.

Whose broad stripes and bright stars, . . .

I felt kind of guilty. It was the first time I could remember ever moving during the National Anthem.

O'er the ram-parts we watched, . . .

My foot kept slipping. The fence wire was eating my fingers to the bone. I had to get over and down before the song ended.

And the rock-ets' red glare, . . .

I got one sneak on top, actually dug it into a barb to help haul the rest of me up. I was there, teetering. It was high.

. . . the bombs burst-ing . . .

A lot higher than I had thought.

. . . in air, . . .

Don't panic. This is the critical moment. One false move

> *Gave proof . . .*

and you're cole slaw.

> *. . . through the night . . .*

I let one leg dangle as far down as possible, steadied myself,

> *. . . that our flag . . .*

and pushed off.

> *. . . was still there: . . .*

Ripping sound. I jerked to a stop. But I wasn't down —

> *O say, . . .*

I was up. The ground still way below my feet. Pressure under my arms. My jacket tight, tugging upward. It was caught on the fence top.

> *. . . does tha-at star-span-gled . . .*

I'm hanging from the fence!

> *. . . ban-ne-er ye-et wa-ave . . .*

I tried to reach back. Couldn't. It was like a full nelson. Why didn't they ever play more than one verse of the National Anthem?

. . . and the home of the brave?

Suddenly everything started moving again, like a stuck movie restarting. A couple thousand people — none of them noticing me yet — just going about their business. Even the guard wasn't turning around. In fact, he was walking away. Great!

"Hi, Jason."

Somebody behind me, outside the fence. I cranked my head around — it would only go a couple inches because of the full nelson the fence had on me — and strained my eyeballs downward. It was the seventh-grader with the Rudolph belt. I wondered how he knew my name.

"What're you doing up there?"

"Beat it!" I hissed. "I'm part of the band show. Beat it! You'll spoil it!"

He left. Then I got noticed by somebody in front of me. A little kid. Real little. He wandered over and stopped right below me. The top of his head didn't come up to my dangling feet. He was munching on a soft pretzel as big as his face. He had a yellow mustache from the mustard. Where was his father? Damn parents, they don't watch their kids.

He held the pretzel up to me. "Want some?"

"No thanks," I said, trying to sound natural. "You better go find your daddy. Aren't you scared?"

He ripped off a huge chunk and stuffed it all in. He shook his head no.

"Well," I said, "I'll bet your daddy's looking for

you right now. The game's gonna start any second. You better hurry up to your seat. *Hurry.*"

He wandered off — straight toward the guard. He tugged at the guard's shirt and said something to him. Just then a man showed up — the negligent father — and snatched the kid away. But the damage was done. The guard was turning, looking, coming . . .

His walk was funny. A waddle. When he got to me, he just stood there with his hands on his hips. At the far end of the field the ball jumped off the grass, tumbled above the crowd, the school, into the night sky — kickoff! At first I thought it might come all the way to me, but it fell to earth in front of the goalpost, and the players were swarming. One thing for sure: you got a great view from where I was.

The guard still didn't say anything. His face just sort of puffed up and twisted, and some gurgly noises came out. Then he waddled off. Great, I thought. Maybe he thinks I'm a dummy somebody hung on the fence. Part of a BEAT RADNOR! float.

He came back, this time with another man, teacher-type. Now two of them were staring up at me. Not to mention other people gawking, pointing, screeching.

"I've seen it all," the teacher finally said.

"Was I right, Mr. Crimmins?" said the guard, not taking his eyes from me. "Was it worth coming over?"

The teacher nodded. "It was. Indeed. I guess he's mortified enough by now. Let's get him down."

Two kids in the long-jump pit were laughing and pointing.

I felt myself grabbed, lifted and unhitched, lowered to the grass. For a split instant I was sorry to be down — I was little again.

The teacher had his hand on my shoulder. "You go to the junior high, son?"

"Yeah." My armpits were killing me.

"Okay. I'm going to let you go now. I think you'll have enough price to pay when your parents see that jacket." He flicked his thumb. "Vamoose."

I vamoosed.

First Half

The announcer was saying, "And that's the end of the first quarter," by the time I finally found the others. They were over on the Radnor side. Dugan and Rich were standing at the rope right in front of the Radnor cheerleaders, so close they could practically spit on them. Peter was down the track a ways, watching the game.

The band was playing a swingy, bebop song, and the cheerleaders were making moves that I saw in the movies but never on a football field. The stands behind us were going crazy. Whistling, stomping. At the finish, the cheerleaders did a really nasty hip-doodle, kicked their legs up high like they were punting, whirled around, bent over, flipped their skirts up and did a quick wiggle-wiggle at the stands. At *us*. What a sight, ten butts in a row! Pandemonium.

Dugan had a box of Cracker Jacks. He wetted a piece in his mouth, and when the cheerleader closest to us bent over, he pitched it and hit her right between the first and second wiggle. Not only that —

26

it stuck, like a caramel barnacle on her Radnor maroon underwear.

The cheerleader's hand shot back; she picked off the Cracker Jack, whipped around, and came stomping and steaming right for us. Except it was no longer us — it was just me, because Dugan and Richie were haul-assing around the track. I froze. I saw the cheerleader's hand coming, but I couldn't move. It got me on the side of the face, and the whole world twitched. A dial tone went off in my head. Suddenly the whole Radnor side erupted with screaming and drums. Were they cheering the cheerleader who hit me?

I had to get to the other side. Friendly territory. But I couldn't make it. I felt myself cracking, crumbling. I groped my way to the end of the enemy stands. I went behind them. Under them. And started bawling. Like my eyes were throwing up. I couldn't stop. I kept feeling that hand on my face, myself on the fence, the hole in my jacket. On and on.

Then I got mad. I wished we could do it all over again. Only this time I would snatch her hand just before it got to my face, and I would snicker-sneer, "Seeya later, baby," and my right fist would come up from somewhere south of Texas and crunch into the underside of her Radnor High School jaw with a shot that would lift her clear off the ground and send her flying into the players' bench. That's what

I kept thinking as I crouched deep in the shadows and wiped my eyes and nose and yanked up fistfuls of grass. The foot-stomping above was deafening, but I wasn't going back out into the light until my face was ready. Then I heard them — voices, a he and a she.

"Here?"

"No."

"Here?"

"Where?"

"Here."

"Okay . . . Owww!"

"What?"

"I hit my head."

"Don't worry about it."

They were behind me. Close.

"Oh, honey."

"You taste good."

"Do I?"

"Yeah."

Real close. I couldn't believe they didn't see me. I tried not to breathe.

"No," she said.

"Come on," he said.

"*No*. I told you. That's the one thing I can't *do*."

"Why not?"

"I can't get messed *up*."

"Why not?"

"Howie, I have to be back in exactly two minutes."

"So, come on."

"I said *no*."

"Shit."

"Howie, there's lots of other things . . . a minute and a half . . . Howie, we don't have all night. Do *some*thing to me."

They stopped talking. They were doing something. But what? My eyes ached all the way down to my stomach. I tried to turn my neck, real slow, but it wouldn't go far enough. I wished I were an owl. My thighs were killing me. I was in a baseball-catcher's crouch, and it was all I could do to keep from toppling forward or backward. I could hear sounds, kind of like somebody eating an ice-cream cone.

Then I remembered what she had said. The minute and a half had to be almost up. What if they came out my way, bumped right into me? I had already been massacred enough for one night. I didn't think any more about it — I bolted. I heard a yelp behind me, but I was flying, down the back of the stands and out into the blazing lights.

I slipped onto an end seat. Pretty soon they came out. He was just regular-looking, but she had on a uniform, long maroon skirt, pure white gloves, white boots with tassels. They split, like they didn't even know each other. He headed off toward the Avon Oaks side, she headed for the Radnor band section. She had to hurry, because the band was already coming down to line up for halftime. She grabbed a tall maroon hat with a white plume — like all the others — and a white rifle and ran down to the far corner of the field.

Second Half

I found Richie and Dugan by the bike rack, checking out the girls going in and out of the restroom. They were smoking. Both started over the summer. Richie buys, Dugan bums.

I told them what happened under the Radnor stands. "That's the one." I pointed to the band coming onto the field. "Next to the American flag."

"Damn," said Richie.

"Banzai," said Dugan.

"What do you think they were doing?" said Richie.

"I told you I don't know," I said. "I couldn't see them."

"So how do you know they were doing *any*thing?"

"Why do *you* think they were under the stands? To work on a book report?"

"All I'm saying is, what do you *think?*"

"What I *know* is, whatever they were doing, they were doing standing up."

"Banzai."

"And he said she tasted good."

"Ban*zai!*"

"And whatever it was, it only took two minutes — no, less."

"How's that?"

"Because she had to get back to the band."

Richie flipped his cigarette butt into a window well. "I don't know, man. Two minutes. How much could they do in two minutes?" He tapped out another 'rette. "Waddaya think, Doog?"

Dugan opened his mouth as if to sing, and a little gray cloud of smoke came out; but before it had a chance to escape, he sucked it up into his nose. When he finally spoke, it came out his mouth, in two syllables: "Depends."

The Radnor band was heading our way. Without a word the three of us dashed for the rope, to get as close to the color guard as we could. She went marching by, about twenty yards away, under the flag, knees pumping high, boot tassels flapping, staring straight ahead, the chin strap practically in her teeth.

"Damn," said Richie.

"Banzai," whispered Dugan.

When the second half started, we were under the Radnor grandstand.

"They gotta come back," Richie said.

"Look, man," I told him, "if they don't come back, that doesn't mean it didn't happen. Don't try to say that."

"This was the spot?"

"Yeah, here."

We were crouching. The cigarettes were out. With

the stomping and yelling and horns above us, it was like being two feet beneath a thunderhead.

"And if they come," I said, "she won't have her hat on."

They never showed up. But something else did. It fell onto Dugan's shoulder. He howled, fumbled around in the dark, and picked it up. "Feels like a can," he said. "Beer?"

We duck-waddled toward the light.

"It is!"

"Miller's!"

A voice called down. "Hey — throw that back up here!"

The three of us looked at each other — and took off. As we raced behind the stands, we kept tossing the can to each other, hot-potato. I wound up with it when we came out front, so I quick took off my jacket and wrapped the can in it. All the way over to the Avon Oaks side, passing guards and teachers and policemen, I knew how smugglers feel.

We went under the home team stands. Richie took the can, held it up. "Got us some brew, baby. Still a little cold, too. Feel."

We felt. It didn't seem cold to me.

"Okay," said Rich, "who's opening?"

"Go ahead," I said. "You're holding it."

"Doog?"

"All yours."

Richie snapped the can open. It hissed like a snake. The air got faintly sour. He held the can up to his nose — "Mmm" — then to our noses. Dugan nodded, pulled the 'rettes from Rich's pocket, lit one.

"Okay," said Rich, "who's first?" He held the can out to me.

Now, I'm not a big beer drinker. In fact, up till then, I wasn't *any* kind of beer drinker. I can only remember having a sip once, and my mother almost killing the uncle who gave it to me.

"Go ahead," I told him. "You opened it."

"Herk, you ain't getting outta here without guzzlin' some of this."

"I'll guzzle what I want. I just ain't crazy about warm beer."

"This ain't warm."

"It ain't cold, either."

"So, it's cool."

"They drink it warm in Mexico," said Dugan.

"Yeah, see that." Richie poked me with the can. "You think you're better'n a Mexican?"

"This beer ain't warm. It's cool. You just said so."

"So?"

"So, cool's the worst. Maybe we oughta wait a while to let it warm up."

He poked — "You just don't wanna take any. You're —" and poked — "weaselin' —" and poked — "out —" and poked.

I smacked the can. "Poke me again, you're a dead man."

Dugan snatched the can and guzzled. He had the cigarette and the can in the same hand. It was impressive. At the end of the guzzle, he held the can out and went, "Ahhhh."

Richie took the can, wiped off the top, and went at it. He did an "Ahhhh" too at the end, but not as good as Dugan.

He held the can to me. I took it. I wiped. I guzzled. I choked. I coughed it out.

"Hey, man!" Richie snatched the can back. "Waddaya trying to do? That's good brew."

"Toldja . . ." I croaked, "I like . . . it cold."

"Here," he said.

He was holding out his cigarettes to me.

"Huh?"

"Take one." He shook the pack — one popped up. I stared at it. "C'mon, man. Look." He took the cigarette out, tapped it on his thumbnail, lit it, and held it out to me.

"Germs," I said.

He shook out another. "Okay, you do it."

"I'm in training," I said.

"For what?"

"Baseball."

"You're just a pussy. You're afraid Marcy's gonna find out."

I took the cigarette.

Dugan took a snort of beer. "Party time!"

So we partied under the foot-stomping, echoing grandstand. It was tall, the can, taller than soda cans, and we kept passing it back and forth, and it lasted and lasted, through the fight songs and the touchdowns and the announcer saying, "That's the end of the third quarter."

Dugan peered into the dark hole of the can. "It keeps being there. It's like the miracle of the fishes."

For a while, none of us said much. We just puffed and swigged. I tried to be careful. Everything that went into my mouth — beer, smoke — I sipped. We were sitting down. The beer went to my stomach, and the smoke went to my lungs and my eyes and my head. Pretty soon it was all mixed together, beer and smoke. I was full of it. Even my feet. Then Dugan turned the can upside down over his face, and when nothing came out, we started laughing. We couldn't stop.

Richie draped his arm around me. "How's it feel, buddy?"

"How's what feel?"

"Tyin' a load on."

"Really?"

"Damn straight, baby. You're drunk. We're all drunk."

"Y'think so?"

"As a skunk."

I stood up. I *was* a little wobbly. I bumped against a grandstand support. I felt . . . smoky. Sleepy, actually. Me. Drunk. As a skunk. I couldn't get over it.

"You sure?" I said.

"You're polluted."

Stampede above us. The game was over. Everybody was leaving.

We bumped into Peter outside the gate.

"Where were you guys?" he said.

"Under the stands," I said.

"*Under?*"

"Yeah. Boozin'."

"Sure you were."

"I ain't kiddin' ya. We were drinking Miller's. Weren't we?"

Rich and Dugan nodded. "We got smashed," I told him.

He sneered. "Right."

"We did. I'm polluted." To prove it, I wobbled. He laughed. "I can't even walk a straight line," I told him.

"You're not drunk," he said with this know-it-all voice, like a parent or doctor.

"Look . . . I'm tryin' to walk the line."

"You're not drunk, Jason."

"I'm almost outta my gourd . . . look."

"Forget it."

"Look!"

He started walking away, when the seventh-grade Rudolph-belt nerd runt appeared in front of me with a couple of his nerd pals. "Hey, Jason," he went, all thrilly, "you drunk?"

"As a skunk," I said. He looked at his nerd pals, all proud of himself. He held out his hand for me to slap, but I was calling after Peter: "Yuh hear that? I'm bombed! *Puh-loooooo-tid!*"

To prove it some more, I draped my arms around my pals, Richie and Dugan, and we went hooting and laughing and wobbling through the streets of Avon Oaks. I'd had one-third of a can of Miller's and nine drags on cigarettes, and nobody was gonna take that away from me.

Sober

It must have been one of those drunks that hit you real hard but don't last too long. By the time Richie and Dugan peeled off to their houses, I could feel myself starting to unpollute. By the time I reached my front door, I was stone-cold sober.

I made the mistake of passing my cootyhead sister on the way up the stairs. She was in her pajamas.

"Eeeewww!" she shrieked. "Mom! *Mah-ahm!*"

Instantly my mother was there. "What, for God's sake?"

"Smell him!" cackled Cootyhead. "*Smell* him!" She was backing away, probably reading my thoughts.

My mother leaned in, her nose twitching like a rabbit's. "What do I smell?"

"Cigarette smoke! He was smoking!"

Cootyhead had backed all the way up the stairs. She was hunched over, her beak jutting out, her bare claws curled over the top step. Vulture.

My mother didn't say anything for a long time, just stared at me. Finally words came out. "Were you smoking?" Somehow she made the last word sound like "stealing" or "murdering."

"I don't smoke," I said. "That's from all the other people at the game."

The vulture squawked: "Smell his breath, Mom! Other people's smoke doesn't hang around inside your mouth!"

I lunged — "I'm gonna kill her —" but my mother blocked the way.

Ham, my stepfather, flashed across the hallway above, holding a rolled-up newspaper. That meant he was chasing moths. Ham believes in life. So he lets spiders alone, and he'll take an hour to herd a horsefly out a window. Last year he thought the little white moths that showed up in the bathroom were kind of cute. Then he started finding holes in his sweaters and jackets. He doesn't think they're so cute anymore.

"Honey, look here," he called, "there's a million of 'em."

My mother didn't seem to hear him. "Let's see your breath, Jason," she said.

"You can't see breath."

"Don't be funny. Open your mouth." I opened. "Breathe."

"I ahn."

"He's holding his breath, Mom!"

"Be *quiet*. Now, breathe on me."

I breathed. She sniffed. Her eyelids fluttered. She was stumped.

"God, Mom! I can tell from up here! It's beer! *Beer!*"

From above, a loud *whack!* of paper club against wall. "Aha! Mothman gotcha!"

"Breathe for me again." Her voice was soft, calm. She cocked her head, as if she was smelling with her ear. I breathed again. She was still stumped. Cootyhead groaned.

"Ham," my mother called.

Whack! "Mothman!"

"*Ham!*"

"Hello?"

"Come here, please."

"Just a sec." *Whack!* "Mothman!"

My mother's eyes were glistening; she closed them. "Please!"

In a couple seconds Ham was alongside her. A small, dead moth was in his hair. He held the club ready, his eyes scanning the ceiling. "What now?"

"Do you smell anything?"

He sniffed, nodded. "Mm . . . yes . . ." He nosed in closer to me. "Yes . . . *yes!*" He was going wild, sniffing me up and down like a pack of hounds. The dead moth tumbled from his head.

"Well?"

He straightened up. "Anchovies. This person has been rolling in anchovy paste." A final sniff. "Recently."

"My mother slumped against the stairway wall. "Lord help us."

"He was smoking and drinking!" Cootyhead screeched. "He's smashed out of his *mind!*"

My mother sighed. "Make her go to her room."

"Mary, go. Room."

She went to her room, closed the door.

"She's still listening," I told them.

"He's been smoking," my mother said.

Ham nodded. "Probably has."

"Now will you check his breath, please."

He checked.

"Well?"

His eyes left the ceiling and landed on me. "Beer, I'd say."

My mother sagged to a seat on the steps.

"Do we have to stay on the stairway?" I said.

Ham's eyes went roaming again. "Does Marceline know you're a drunk?"

"I'm not drunk. If you don't believe me, call Peter Kim. Go ahead. I'll give you his number."

My mother rested her head against the wall, closed her eyes. "It's starting."

"Honey," said Ham, leaning over the railing, "you've been saying that for years now. Seems to me, whatever 'it' is —" *whack!* — "gotcha! — we must be pretty deep into it by now."

"Smoking. Drinking."

Cootyhead's door sprang open — "He curses, too!" — and slammed shut.

Ham flicked a moth corpse from the paper club. "He's a regular Prince of Darkness."

Another door opened, and there was the face of little Timmy, all scrunched and blinky in the hallway light. "What's the noise?" he whined.

"Back in your room," my mother ordered. "This is not for children."

Timmy rubbed his eyes. "Jason's a children."

"Ham."

Ham took Timmy back to his bed. My mother waited till he came back. "This is how it starts. It's not just the cigarettes and the beer per se, although that's bad enough. It's the smoking and the drinking. What do you smoke next? What do you drink next?"

Whack! "Mothman!"

"Stop *iiiit!*"

This is the way it usually goes — my mother all tragic, Ham cool. He has sort of made peace with us kids. In fact, he claims to be the founding father and only member of Parents' Organization of Peace (POOP).

"Honey, look," he said, "the kid's been pretty good, day in and day out. He does well in school. He comes in on time. He washes his feet. What more can you ask?"

"I ask him to grow up to be a decent human being, that's all. I don't demand A's, just decency."

"Fine. He's on his way. Decent doesn't mean perfect. Let's give him some slack. If we don't, he'll snap the line and run."

I felt my mother's hand on my shoulder, squeezing; then it jerked away. "Oh no! Jason."

"What?"

"What's this?"

"What's what?"

"This hole in your jacket." She was sticking her

finger through it. "What in the *name* of . . . were you *doing* tonight?"

"It got stuck."

"*Stuck?*"

"Yeah."

"What do you mean stuck? Stuck on what?"

"A fence."

"A fence? Jason, that's a good jacket. How could you do that?"

"Probably trying to sneak in," said Ham.

She cupped my jaw in her hand and pulled my face around, like I was in third grade. "Jason, what *else* were you doing tonight?"

I just stared at her.

"I think I know," said Ham. "I think I can cut right to the bottom of all this. Jason, look at me." I looked at him. "Now answer me, because this is all that really matters. This will prove your innocence. Who — won — the — game?"

I just stared at him.

A leaking air kind of sound came from my mother's mouth. She got up, stepped over me, and went downstairs. A minute later I could hear her doing things in the kitchen.

Bedroom

At first, when I heard the doorbell ring, I wondered who could be coming so early on a Saturday
morning. Then I opened my eyes and looked at the
clock. It was already after nine. I closed my eyes.
I was groggy. Was it from sleep? Or the beer and
smoke? The voices downstairs drifted in and out of
my grog. It wasn't until the front door closed that
I realized who it was. I jumped up, ran to the window, and threw it open. She was already pedaling
up the sidewalk.

"Marceline!"

She stopped, pushed herself backward a few rev-
olutions, waved. "IIi!"

"Where're you going?"

"Oh, just riding." She slid down from the seat.

"Was that you just here?"

"Uh-huh."

"What did you want?"

"I was giving your mother a recipe."

"What for?"

"Cookies."

I was disappointed. I thought maybe she had

stopped by to see me. She wore her shades and her painter's cap and a hooded sweatshirt that I had never seen before. I couldn't put my finger on the color — a kind of rosy-pink-orange, like a ray from the roof-high sun had snagged itself on her. I couldn't think of anything to say. I crouched so that only my head was above the windowsill. I didn't want my pajamas to show.

"That a new sweatshirt?"

"No, it's old."

Her right foot was fishing back for its pedal.

"I never saw it."

"I never wear it."

Her foot found the pedal. She was back on the seat.

"It's nice."

"Thank you. Jason —"

"Missed a great game last night."

"Jason, I have to be going. Call me up later, okay?"

She was gone.

"Okay!" I yelled, standing up.

When I asked my mother about the cookie recipe, she started to grin. "That girl . . . a pretty sharp cookie herself. That's what she told you? Cookie recipe?"

"So what was it really?"

"I guess I'm allowed to tell you. Walk for Hunger."

"She signed you up?"

"Right under your nose. Guess she knew you hadn't bothered to ask us yet."

Walk for Hunger is a school thing. High school and junior high. Help feed the starving people in Africa. You ask people to pledge a certain amount, whatever they want, for each mile you walk, up to ten miles. The three junior-high grades are supposed to compete against each other, see who makes the most. Marceline is student chairman for ninth grade.

"Wha'd you sign up for?" I said.

"Fifty cents a mile. There's another fifty a mile available if you're interested."

I just grunted and went back upstairs.

It was almost lunchtime when I finally spotted Marceline's bike outside a house on Braeburn. I stayed across the street. In a minute she came out. She took a little notepad from her sunrise sweatshirt and wrote something in it.

I called: "Cookies, huh?"

She looked up, grinned. "Early bird gets the pledge." She put the notepad away and coasted over.

"That's pretty dirty. My own parents."

"You had first crack at them. You blew it."

"Who said I blew it? Why should I get pledges if I'm not even walking?"

The foxy grin disappeared. She swung her front wheel into my front wheel. I had to hold my wheel rigid against the pressure. "Herkimer, you *are* walking."

"Mm, maybe a mile or two."

"Try ten."

It was one of those rare times — the light was right, I was close enough — when I could see her freckles. Each time it happens, I'm surprised, and happy, to find them still there. It's like they're invisible to everyone but me. Her only makeup. I couldn't admit it to her, but I would have walked a hundred miles if she told me to.

"Want me to buy you lunch?" I said. "Two hot dogs for ninety-nine cents at 7-Eleven this week."

She smiled, backed off; the freckles vanished. "It's a deal."

As we pushed off down the street, she turned the grin back on. "Why were you hiding under the window up there? Didn't want me to see your jammies?"

"Bet they're cuter than yours."

"Who said," she grinned, "I wear jammies to bed?"

My mind, for the next half hour, was definitely not on the ride to 7-Eleven. Or the hot dog. Or the Slurpee that we shared.

After lunch she gave me half of her pledge slips and assigned me one side of Colfax while she took the other.

"You're really out to beat the other grades, aren't you?" I said.

"I'm really out to feed a few people," she said.

We covered all of Colfax plus two blocks of Harrington, when we ran out of pledge slips. We rode back to her house for more.

I was just sitting down on the living-room sofa when she said, "Come on up," and trotted upstairs.

Was she talking to me? I looked around. I peeked into the kitchen. Nobody else seemed to be home. I headed for the stairs the way I would close in on a large, dark hole in the woods. I put one foot up on the first step. "Marceline —" I called, "did you say for me to come up?"

"Yes, yes." She sounded a little impatient.

As I went up, I kept looking down. With each step I half expected her father to burst around a corner bellowing, "Where do you think *you're* going?" But the only sound was my own footsteps, like faint puffs on the blue-carpeted stairs.

I made it. The first doorway I peeked into was a bathroom. Then a bedroom, empty.

"Jason!"

I jumped. She was standing in a doorway behind me. "Are you coming, or would you rather go sneaking around my house?"

When I went in she was holding up a handmade poster. Huge. It showed different-colored feet walking across a bridge to Africa. It said, HUNGER IS JUST A TEN-MILE WALK FROM HERE . . . 9TH GRADERS, SUPPORT THE WALK FOR HUNGER!

"What do you think?" she said.

"Okay," I said. "Great."

"I got permission to put it on the door of the ninth-grade office. And" — she hauled out another poster; this one showed a bunch of happy kids getting food and said, THE PLURAL OF MILES IS SMILES . . . WALK ON, 9TH GRADERS! — "this one in the cafeteria."

"Super," I said, but I wasn't really paying attention. All I could think was: Man, I'm in her bedroom! Marceline McAllister's bedroom! Unbelievable! And not a parent in sight!

It had a bed and a dresser and a mirror and a desk and a chair and a closet and a bookcase and a music stand and two gray, fluffy slippers that didn't look like slippers but like a pair of little hippos with their mouths wide open ready to devour any foot that came their way. My eyes swung back to the music stand. Something was dangling from it . . . something white . . . a bra! I was getting woozy. Then her hands were on my shoulders, turning me around to face her. She was close, her hands on my chest, my shirt, close, her freckles big as cornflakes . . . My God! She's moving on me! This is it!

"Ah —" she went, "there." She backed away, staring at my chest. "How's that?"

I looked down. A red button about twice the size of a quarter was pinned to my pocket. There was white lettering. I twisted my pocket so I could read: *I Walked for Hunger.*

"Everybody that walks will get one," she said.

"I didn't walk yet."

"That's right." She pulled the button off. "Just testing."

She showed me the rest of her Walk stuff, and then we went downstairs and had some orange juice and got back on our bikes and did some more streets. When I left to go home, she said she was staying out to knock off another block or two. She asked if I'd like to come over after dinner to see a movie on their VCR. I said sure.

I let my bike find its way home, like a horse. All I could think of were the bedroom and the bra. What was it doing there? She could have quick grabbed it, stuck it somewhere out of sight, hid it from me. Why didn't she? One thing for sure: she didn't mind me seeing it. She knew it was there, and she knew I would see it, and she didn't try to stop me from seeing it. And how about her parents not being home? And that crack, "Who said I wear jammies to bed?" Did it all add up to something? To what?

It started to dawn on me that maybe I had blown it. I mean, a girl waits till her parents are out of the house, then takes you home with her and tells you to come up to her bedroom. Come on, Herkimer, waddaya need, a gold-plated invitation? She set the whole thing up. She tried to make it easy for you, even used the red button as an excuse to get close. She was waiting for you to make your move — and what did you do? Nothing. Zero. Zip.

Dumb-ass.

Babysitting

When I got back to Marceline's, her parents' car was in the driveway. I was trying to figure out how I felt about that when she came bopping out of the house.

"Park your bike," she said. "We're walking."

"Walking? Where? What about the movie?"

She looked at her watch, pulled my arm. "We're babysitting. Come on. We have to be there in five minutes."

Babysitting!

Bells. Fireworks. Lightning bolts.

". . . the Crenshaws," she was saying. "They called just a little while ago. They have a little boy, a baby . . ."

Her voice kept fading out. *Babysit.* I had heard it all. Girl gets babysitting job. Boyfriend tags along. Or sneaks in after people leave. Whole place to themselves. Stereo. Refrigerator. Sofa. Rug. Your own apartment. For hours. It was classic. It was how people got together. More room than on a car seat. Softer than your basement. Cleaner than the ground. No bugs. No oil stains. Fifty, maybe sixty percent of everything that guys get is gotten at babysitting.

I kept thinking: You're going babysitting. Yeah, you. See the girl walking alongside you — the sort of tall one, straw-colored hair, light freckles, tiny chip out of one front tooth, foxy? Well, she's going babysitting and she wants you to go with her. In a matter of minutes you're going to be inside somebody's house, with her, yeah, with that girl, the girl right next to you. Last night a beer. This afternoon a bedroom, a bra. Tonight . . .? Welcome to the fast lane, dude.

"This one," she said.

Up the walk, up the steps, knock-knock — we were in. The mother was all hyper. "Oh, Marceline, I'm so glad you could come. We haven't been out since the baby was born. Is this your friend you mentioned? Boyfriend?" Silence, blushing. "Ah —" patting her lips — "big mouth. None of my business." Showing Marceline the diapers, the milk, the stove. "Do you know how to check if it's warm enough? On the *inside* of your wrist." (She knew.) "You don't think we're terrible, do you, leaving a four-month-old baby. We haven't gone out to so much as the drugstore since Rory was born. I'm glad your friend's a boy. I'll feel even better now."

"Claire, good-bye?" called the husband, who had been standing by the door the whole time. He left.

The wife finally followed ("The fridge is yours. Take anything you want. Anything. Hear? Jason?") after the second toot from the car horn.

Marceline closed the door. And locked it. For protection? Or privacy?

This was it. Before the night was over, one of two things was going to happen: either she was going to make a move, or I was going to make a move. I couldn't wait to find out. Or could I?

"That," she said, turning from the door, "is one stupendous sofa."

It was. Maybe the biggest sofa I had ever seen. Took up one whole wall. Tan-and-white job. Pillowy. Long enough for a couple of six-footers to lie down on. Was that where the move was going to take place? Or would it happen on the rust-colored rug? Or in another room?

She sat down. I sat down. "Better call your parents," she said. I got up. "Tell them you're here instead of my place."

The phone was in the kitchen. Cootyhead answered, all breathless and interested until she heard who it was; then the receiver went *donk!* against something as she dropped it the way she would if she had picked up a dead rat by mistake. I knew it was fifty-fifty whether she would bother to tell anyone I was on the phone. After a week or two, Timmy came to the phone. He wanted me to tell him what was wrong with the paper airplane he made. Finally Ham got on. He wasn't much better.

"Babysitting, huh? Likely story."

"Why? What do you think we're doing?"

He snickered. "I know what goes on during baby-sitting."

"Yeah, we sit on the baby."

"I'm checking you for hickeys when you get home."

"Good-bye."

As soon as I hung up, Marceline came in. Holding the baby. The baby was wearing a mini-nightshirt, which I thought was kind of sissy, since it was supposed to be a boy baby. Two tiny, pink feet were sticking out.

"Goodness *gway*-shuss," Marceline said to the baby, "that certainly was a looooong phone call, wasn't it?" She sounded just like mothers I've heard. She turned the baby toward me. "Rory, this is Jason. Jason, say hello to Rory."

I was getting uncomfortable. I'm not used to being around babies. I never paid much attention to Timmy till he was about three. The kid's eyes were gaping at me like they didn't believe what they saw. His face was kind of twitching this way and that, and he was blowing tiny bubbles with his own spit. I used to get hollered at for doing it with a straw.

"Hello," I said.

She turned the kid to herself. "Did you hear *that?* Hel-*lo?* What kind of greeting was *that?* He didn't even shake him's hand!" She rubbed noses with him and turned him back to me. She held his hand out. "Say, 'Shake my hand, Jason.' "

I was liking this less and less. I stuck out my finger. The kid took one swipe at it, then he grabbed it and started pulling on it, like he wanted it. So I let him have it, and next thing I know, my finger's in his mouth and he's chomping away on it with his gums.

I yanked my finger out. "Hey, man, cool it." I wiped off the baby spit.

Marceline eskimoed him again. "Hey, man, cool it," she mimicked in a low, gruff voice. "Now what kind of way is that to speak to a wittle fella? Just because him's getting his toofers and wants something to chew on." She gave him one of her knuckles, which he started gnawing on like it was a T-bone steak. "We didn't like his old finger anyway, did we?"

"Funny kind of pajamas for a boy," I said.

She lifted it up, showing diapers. "It's a nightgown."

"For a boy?"

She lifted him over her head so that he was looking down at her. She carried him into the living room. "My, my, Mister Herkimer doesn't like our little nightgown, does he? Mister Herkimer is one tough dude, I'm telling you. He's a straight-shootin', rootin-tootin son-of-a-gun, and he ain't gonna put up with nooooo baby boys wearing nightgowns in *his* town, no siree, not while *he's* sheriff."

She turned on the radio and started dancing with him. I never knew she could dance. She never danced with me. But then, I never danced with anybody.

"What kinda name's that, anyway?" I said. "Rory."

"It's a perfectly fine name," she said-sang, swinging to the music. "Isn't it? Ror-ee, Ror-ee, give me your answer do — I'm half . . . half . . ."

"Gory," I supplied.

". . . gor-ee, Over the love of youuuuu . . ." She stopped, looked at her hand. "Uh-oh."

"What's the matter?"

"I think he's wet."

"Don't look at me. That's your department."

"Did you hear that, Rory? My department. He doesn't want to feedum him's finger. He doesn't want to make-um dry. He doesn't have *any* department. Aunt Marceline has alllllll the departments."

She laid him down on the rust-colored rug. On his back, right in the middle of it. I didn't like the looks of this. I thought these things were supposed to happen in the bathroom, or the bedroom. I moseyed off, figured I'd check out the refrigerator.

"Jason," she called.

"Huh?"

"Go get me some diapers, please."

"I don't know where they are." I opened the fridge. Pretty good stock. Grape juice looked okay.

"They're in the dining room."

I opened the freezer. "What dining room?" Bon Bons!

"Jason."

"Soon's I get a little bite here. Want a Bon Bon?"

"You have five seconds."

"She said the refrigerator's ours."

"— two — three —"

I got the diapers. By now she had the kid naked except for the nightgown, which was up around his neck. As I walked over, he turned his head to me and stuck his two little bowlegs in the air and grinned. I tried not to look.

She took the diapers. "See, he likes you."

"Wait'll he gets to know me."

"Here."

She was holding something up to me. White. Crumply. Saggy. Soggy. Between two fingers.

"Oh no," I said.

"Jason, take it. Just throw it in the wastebasket in the kitchen."

"I don't deal with diapers. Especially those kind."

"It's only a little wet."

"I'll bet."

"Grow up, Jason." She reached across the kid, grabbed my wrist, and pulled it toward her. She held the dirty diaper in front of my clamped hand. "I'm not letting go till you take this. Now see, hold it here, where it's dry, just with your fingerti—"

There was no sound, no warning — but there *was* a thin, pale-yellow stream, and it was shooting almost straight up into the air, like a fountain at the mall, a good two feet or more — I couldn't believe the height he was getting — and maybe the stream would have shot even higher (the ceiling?) if something hadn't been in its way, like my arm. It felt all warm, like bathwater. He was still grinning.

By the time I came out of my shock and yanked my arm away, Marceline was rolling on the rug, laughing herself red in the face. The geyser came down, as though somebody had taken his foot off a water-fountain pedal, and finally petered out on the rust-colored rug. I couldn't think of anything to say except, "He *pissed* on me!" Which sent Marceline into more spasms.

I went into the kitchen and scrubbed my arm for five minutes with the rough side of a dish pad and some lemon-smelling soap. When I went back, she was waiting with two eyes filled with laugh tears and a hand dangling the diaper. "You *still* didn't take this."

I did an about-face, got the basket from the kitchen, brought it to her, and let her drop it in.

Then she wanted me to go look for baby powder. I finally found the baby powder. Then it was some kind of ointment she wanted.

"Man," I said, "will you just put the damn diaper on before he decides to piss again."

"He has a rash," she snapped. "Forget it. I'll get it myself."

She stomped out and left us alone. I did not like this at all. I did not like being in the same room with a naked baby, especially one that kept swinging its feet toward the ceiling, mooning me — and grinning.

But that wasn't the worst part. The worst part was that I kind of felt like it was a little me there on the rug. It wasn't my grin, and it wasn't my size, but the part between the legs — well, maybe it wasn't really me, but it might as well have been. I mean, there's only two sexes, right? — boys and girls — and from what I've seen, us guys are all pretty much alike. Different sizes maybe, and colors, but the basic stuff, the shape, that's pretty much standard from day one. So it's like, where's the privacy in privates? How can you hide? If one guy in the room has his pants down, everybody's exposed.

Marceline came back with a white tube of glop, which she squeezed onto her finger and proceeded to smear over the kid's butt and even on his tiny tadpole not-so-private privates. I thought she'd be embarrassed, want to get it over with. Wrong. She was taking her good old time, hauling his legs this way and that, gawking all over him, putting little glop dabs on every last speck of rash. My face was burning. The kid was grinning.

Well, at long last it was done. The kid was diapered up, and his nightgown was back down, and there was nothing left for me to do but start praying: *Don't crap.* She picked him up and walked him around from room to room, sometimes dancing to the radio music, always jabbering away at him, the way some people do to their pets.

"Why do you keep talking to him?" I said. "He can't understand."

"I'm getting him ready to talk. If nobody ever said anything to him, he'd never learn." She turned him to me. "Say something to him."

"That's dumb. I don't talk to babies. Where'd you get all this stuff about babies, anyway?"

"I've been babysitting my neighbor's kids since I was twelve. Come on. Just say anything."

"Anything," I said.

"Jason."

I looked the little pisser in the eye. "You're a nerd."

"Terrific," sneered Marceline. "Look at this — you call him a name and what's he do, he gives you a biggum, biggum smile. He really *likes* you."

"My irresistible charm."

She held him out to me. "Here, charmer."

I backed off. "Oh no."

"Stop being a baby."

"I'll stop being a baby when he stops being a baby."

"Jason, hold him. It won't kill you."

"He already pissed on me. I don't wanna find out what's next."

"Just for a minute. Here."

She had me backed up against the front door. She laid him against my shoulder. She lifted one of my hands and placed it under his butt, then she placed my other hand behind his back. Then she took her hands away. How did she know I wouldn't let him drop?

I was holding a baby.

Not a puppy baby. Not a kitten baby. Not a hey-baby-what're-you-doin'-tonight baby. Not a whining-kid crybaby baby. But the real, original thing. A baby person. A *baby* baby.

His bald head kept bumping into my ear. He turned, and his nose brushed my cheek. He smelled powdery. Pink. He blubbled syllables that didn't add up to words. His hand groped across my face. He poked me in the eye. He stuck a finger up my nose. But mostly, he just kept squirming. Not like he wanted to get away, but like he knew he could do whatever he wanted and he wouldn't get dropped. His feet barely made it to my waist. I felt like a giant. Like by not letting him drop, I was keeping him alive. Whether he knew it or not, the little dude needed me. Awesome.

Her hands reached out, took him. "I didn't *give* him to you. I loaned him."

She played with him on the rug for a while. Then the grin on his face started to sag, and then he got jerky, and then he got whiny. Marceline popped up. "Bed and bottle time."

She warmed a bottle in the kitchen, stuck it in his mouth, and hauled him sucking like a champ off to beddy-bye. When she came back, she was holding a dark red box.

"Scrabble!"

Scrabble

We set up the game in the middle of the living-room rug. Seven letter-tiles apiece, first turn mine, because I had drawn the letter closest to the start of the alphabet. It was also my turn to keep score.

When Marceline and I play Scrabble, it's serious business, almost war. The games last forever, because we never lay down our letters until we're sure they're making a word that's worth more points than any other in the English language. We insult each other, and we argue over allowing certain words. The loser usually gets laughed at, and sometimes we don't speak to each other for a day or two afterward.

I opened up with TEAR. Eight points. Crappy letters, crappy start. She topped my R with a T and ran down four more letters for TREBLE, making sure she gave me an evil little snicker as she plunked the B down on a Triple Letter Score space.

"I hate to tell you this," I smirked, "but TREMBLE has an M in it."

"I hate to tell *you* this," she resmirked, "but the word is not TREMBLE, as in 'Jason trembled at the thought of losing yet another Scrabble game to Marceline.' The word, dear boy, is TREBLE, as in music."

"That's what you say."

"Look it up."

We stopped and stared at each other. When we can't agree on a word, the dictionary is the final judge. If it's not in the dictionary, it goes off the board, plus you lose your turn. So you don't say "Look it up" lightly. We looked around. No dictionary.

"Okay," she said, "how about if we write down any words we don't agree on. Tomorrow we look them up, and if anybody played a word not in the dictionary, that person starts the next game fifty points down." She held out her hand. "Agreed?"

"Agreed."

We shook.

"Fourteen points," she said. She leaned over the board to make sure I wrote the number down right.

Fourteen to eight. It never got any closer than that. I played off the L in TREBLE and laid down LET over a Double Word Score square: six points. She hauled out an S, made LETS out of LET, and ran SAW down from there. Two words, sixteen points. I stacked up PINT (seven points) using the T in TEAR. She took my I and with a gleeful squawk dumped an APHID on me, triple-letter-scoring the four-point H.

"Never heard of it."

"It's a bug. Nineteen."

"You're a bug."

"Sticks and stones . . . Nineteen, scorekeeper."

At first I tried, I really did. If not to win, at least
to avoid Total Disgrace, which happens if you lose
by fifty points or more. The closest brush either of
us ever had with it was the time I beat Marceline
by forty-three. She said it was horrible, being that
close to Total Disgrace. She vowed never to let it
happen again and learned twenty new words that
night.

After four or five rounds it got harder and harder
to concentrate on Scrabble. Because Marceline and
I were alone. On the rug. *Babysitting*. And because
of the three voices in the room. One of them was
Marceline's. It was out loud, and it was having a
great ol' time snickering and sneering and mocking
as I fell farther and farther behind in the score. The
other two voices were not out loud. They were in
my head. They were both me, but one of them sounded
suspiciously like Richie.

ME-1: Go for it.

ME-2: Hold it, man. Wait. Not so damn fast.

ME-1: You waited almost fifteen years. Go for it.

ME-2: Go for *what?*

MARCELINE: . . . and M on the Triple Letter. That's
twelve . . . fourteen . . . seventeen . . . eighteen
. . . twenty-one, please, scorekeeper, if you can
count that high.

ME-1: Make your move.

ME-2: *What* move? I don't know how to make a move.

ME-1: Sure you do. It's natural. Like a fish swimming. There's a move inside you trying to get out. Let it out.

ME-2: Let's wait till next week.

ME-1: Life is passing you by.

ME-2: I don't have any experience.

ME-1: Opportunity doesn't wait for experience.

ME-2: I could use some practice. With my pillow.

ME-1: Make it easy on yourself. Pretend she's your pillow.

MARCELINE (*applauding*): Brilliant, Jason, brilliant! A . . . T. AT. I didn't know you knew such long words.

ME-1: You're stalling.

ME-2: She's not ready.

ME-1: The bedroom. The bra. Babysitting. Playing around with the baby. Like she's the *mommy* and you're the *daddy*. Let me put it this way: In the space of only one day, she has arranged to be alone with you in two different houses.

ME-2: Jeez. I never thought of it that way.

ME-1: Go for it.

MARCELINE: Seventeen!

ME-2: I can't.

ME-1: You can.

ME-2: She won't like it.

ME-1: Are you kidding? Look at her. Did you ever see her in a better mood? She's massacring you.

You're making her happier than she's been in weeks. What could spoil that? She's *ripe*.

MARCELINE: Twenty-*threeee!*

ME-2: It's too soon.

ME-1: Wrong, banana brain. It's getting late. It's time to find out exactly what you two are. Just Scrabble palsies? Or more?

ME-2: Maybe I'm afraid to find out.

ME-1: You pathetic moron. You think you have a choice, don't you?

ME-2: Don't I?

ME-1: Hell no. There's only one fact that counts: you are babysitting. You *have* to do something.

ME-2: I can't. I'm not ready.

ME-1: And not only that, you have to do something big. Something worthy of babysitting. Tradition's at stake. What you do in the next couple minutes could determine the rest of your life. You may never get this chance again.

ME-2: I can't.

ME-1: Never again . . . never again . . .

Words zigged and zagged all over the board. We were down to our last rack of tiles. Marceline's eyes rolled up to me, a wicked grin twisted her lips. "Been saving this."

She laid down an I. She placed it on the end row on the side of the board nearest me, on the inside of an E. Then came a B. She was spelling it backwards. So far, BIE. No mystery to what she was doing. She was working her way toward the Fort

Knox of Scrabble, a bright red Triple Word Score space. She laid the letters down real slow, savoring each one. Her eyebrows were dancing. She was humming. Next an M. Going even slower now. Fingering the tiles, caressing them, making them line up perfectly. Even before she laid the O down next to Triple Word Score, I knew she had the Z (worth ten big ones) for ZOMBIE. One of the two most valuable letters, and she was putting it on the most valuable scoring space left. That would be thirty for the Z alone. A bonanza. A Scrabble freak's dream. With a dainty pinch between thumb and forefinger, she lifted the Z from her rack and reached across the board, toward me, zeroing in on the bright red square, leaning over the board . . . leaning . . . leaning . . .

"Can you tell us how it feels, Mister Herkimer, to be in Total Dis—"

I don't know which of us was more surprised when my hand reached out, reached out to her bra and cupped it — the left one — and my mouth made a silly-ass grin and said, "Hi."

Her head snapped up, her eyes big as Frisbees, and that's how we were, eyeballs to eyeballs, her shirt shock-frozen to my hand, when a key came cricketing in the front door, followed by Mrs. Crenshaw's cheery, breathless voice: "We're home!"

Notes

Dear Marceline,
I am writing this note because I hope you will answer it, since you are not talking to me. Maybe it will be easier for you to write. I guess I just have one question. Are you:
    (a) very mad at me?
    (b) totally mad at me?
    (c) break-my-kneecaps mad at me?

           Sincerely Yours,
           Jason

Dear Marceline,
While I am waiting to receive your answer, I thought I would mention that I was thinking that maybe you are bothered by a problem at home, or maybe you have a lot on your mind because of the Walk for Hunger. Maybe it is something I can help you with (with which I can help you??). We always talked

about things before, you know. Well, I hope you can find time to answer this.

Respectfully Yours,
Jason

P.S. Total Disgrace is just as bad as you said it would be. I guess there is just one good thing about it — if somebody had to put me there, I am glad it turned out to be you.

Dear Marceline,
OK, it was a dumb question. I do not blame you for not bothering to answer it. I already know you are mad at me, and I guess I know the reason why too. I guess all I can say is what I said that night. I am sorry. I am not really sure why it happened. (A mystery to me.) I did not think it was going to happen. But then it did. I wish there were some way I could make it not happen. Or unhappen. Remember the space station I made in 7th grade? Maybe I will start working on a time machine. If I finally perfect it, the first thing I will do is climb into it along with you (it will be a 2-seater) and turn it back to that night just before you put down ZOMBIE. Then we could start all over.

Very Sincerely,
Jason

P.S. *Question:* What is worse than Total Disgrace? *Answer:* Having Marceline mad at you.

Dear Marceline,

This is my fourth letter to you. You have just found it in your locker. I am telling you that because maybe you have not looked into your blue binder during the past three days. If you would like to look into your binder now (go ahead, I'll give you time to look) that's where you will find my first three letters. I will not repeat everything I said in them. Just that I would really like to hear from you and start getting along with you again. I am enclosing a piece of paper for your reply in case you ran out.

> *Your Friend,*
> *Jason*

Dear Marceline,

Hi! How's it going? How are things coming along on the Walk for Hunger? Your posters are really great!!! (Everybody says so!!) Guess what I did? Every day after school this week I went around signing up pledges for the WFH. I even went around to the rich people over in Larchmont. If I go all ten miles and everybody pays up I can collect $145.50. And I am not done yet. Sorry if I sound like I am bragging. I just thought you would like to know. Since you are the chairman . . . excuse me . . . chairWOMAN. Like you said, it is the least we can do for all those starving kids.

> *Your Partner Against Hunger,*
> *Jason*

Dear Marceline,

I just had a scary thought. Maybe you are answering my letters but they are not getting to me. Like maybe they are getting lost. Or maybe someone is taking them. Or maybe you are leaving them in some place where I do not look. Or maybe you are afraid somebody might see you slipping them into my locker or books. So I have an idea. Do you know the Avon Deli that you pass on the way home from school, and the big green trash can right outside chained to the parking meter? Well, if you have a letter for me just fold it and slip it under the trash can. Then each day I will make sure I check under the can both on my way to school and coming home. Don't worry. If you leave your letters there, I will get them. For sure.

> *Your "Pen Pal,"*
> *Jason*

Dear Marceline,

Mothers are really wifty sometimes, aren't they. Last night my mother told me that I had to stay off my bike one whole day. (Wow!) Know why? Because somebody told her they saw me riding down Manoa Hill with no hands during rush hour. (Actually it was no feet too.) She said I could have gotten killed (ha-ha). I could have hit a rock and been thrown into the face of an onrushing car. Or maybe a truck. Isn't that crazy? I bet your mother would not worry about such silly stuff. Just thought you would like to hear that story about my wifty mother.

From,
"No Hands Herkimer"
(Jason)

Dear Marceline,

I don't mean to keep bothering you writing to you like this, but I was just thinking that in case you tried to call me last night between 8 and 8:30 and found that you could not reach me, I guess I owe you an explanation. It all started this morning when I noticed a tingeling sensation in my right arm. At first I did not think too much about it. When you are an athlete, you know, you learn to shrug off minor aches and pains. But just for the heck of it I decided to ask Calvin about it. (I did not tell him it was me who had the tingeling.) He said it could possibly be caused by poor circulation, like cholesterol plugging up the veins and all. Or it could be part of the brain going rotten (the part that controls the right arm). Or maybe a malignant tumor. Well, I guess there is not much you can do about brain rot, but I figured if I really am getting lumpy blood I am going to go down fighting. So I went down to Super Fresh to see if they had any health pills or vitamins that could unplug veins, and that is why I was not at home to receive any phone calls between 8 and 8:30 o'clock last night.

Your Friend Forever,
Jason

Dear Marceline,
You are probably wondering what the enclosed piece of paper is. It is an ad from the Sunday magazine about a military academy in Virginia. I wrote them for information and an application form. Ham said it would be "totally swell" if I went. My mother did not say anything. It goes up to junior college. So I could be there until I am 20 (if my blood has not turned to one long rope of fat by then). The ad has the address of the academy in case you would ever like to write me there.

Yours Truly,
Cadet Jason M. Herkimer

P.S.   *Roses are red*
        Violets are blue
        I am not a violet
        But I am blue too

* * *

J.
A tingling sensation in your arm can also come from sleeping on it. Or by not exercising it enough by opening your dictionary to find out how to spell *tingling*.

M.

Africa

I had made a deal with myself. If Marceline stopped being mad, I would do all ten miles of the Walk for Hunger. So, when she finally started speaking to me again (thank you, God), I couldn't use the fact that I had the flu as an excuse not to walk.

The night before, I was bolting for the bathroom every fifteen minutes. By morning I was a limp noodle. I could hardly make it to the breakfast table. How was I going to walk ten miles? The Walk didn't start till 1:00, so I spent the morning lying on the sofa with tea and toast. "Drink lots of fluids," my mother kept telling me. "Diarrhea dehydrates you."

By 12:00 I was still making trips to the bathroom, but my stomach was feeling better. At 12:45 my mother drove me to the high school, where the Walk was supposed to start and finish. She tried to talk me out of going, but I told her I had to. With the money I had pledged to me, I might put ninth grade in first place. She put two dollars in my hand. "Buy things to drink along the way," she said as I got out of the car.

The center of the mob was under a big red-and-white banner stretched between two trees. I found Richie and Calvin and Peter, and we listened to some high-school teacher with a bullhorn give a pep talk, like we were all going out to play a football game or something. Then Marceline called the ninth-graders together and passed out maps of the route and the "I Walked for Hunger" buttons. Then the teacher drew his arm way back and shot it forward like he was heaving a shotput and he bellowed through the bullhorn: "Let's go!" A bunch of cheers went up, mostly from seventh-graders, and we took off.

It was like the start of the Boston Marathon. A million people jamming into one street all at once. Grown-ups were clapping and snapping pictures. From somewhere a football fight song was blaring. Kids were walking backwards, sidewards, moon-walking, boogalooing. One guy was walking on his hands. High-school girls were riding on their boy-friends' shoulders. Seventh-graders were squealing and racing to get to the front of the pack, where the whirling light of a police car was spitting red. I felt a slap on my back, heard a "Hi, Jace!" and saw Rudolph-belt go clomping past, flapping his arm back at me. Almost nobody was just plain walking.

We went up Darby Road to Beech, down Beech to Henderson, down Henderson to Elm, past the bowling lanes. I asked Peter, who was holding the map, how far we had gone.

"Almost two miles," he said.

This is a breeze, I thought.

The mob was strung out by now. From where we were, the beginning and the end of the line were both out of sight. From an airplane we must have looked like army ants on the march. The girls had come down from the guys' shoulders.

I knew Marceline was in the back, with the other people in charge. But there were plenty of other girls around, and some of the best of them, mostly cheerleaders, were bunched along with us and some other guys, mostly football players. We were the main ninth-grade section.

We had a great time.

Britstein, the varsity quarterback, had his football, so we played a moving-field sort of game, half guys, half girls on each team. We ran pass patterns across parking lots and people's lawns.

I was on Britstein's team. A receiver. I'd go zigzagging down the street, scrape my man off on a car or telephone pole, break into the clear, scream for the ball. But Britstein wouldn't throw it. He wasn't even looking for me. It took me just two plays to see he only had eyes for one of his receivers: Jewel Fiorito. She had a green-and-white striped shirt on, and when she ran those stripes did things no stripes ever did before. After a while all the guys on both sides caught on, and the other receivers would slow down and stop, and pretty soon the only player moving in the game was Jewel, with Britstein waving her to go deep, come in, run to the right, the left. A single pass play would last two or three minutes. The game ended about the time Jewel got tired and quit. For the next couple minutes, it was a treat just to watch her breathing heavy.

Then we just kind of messed around. Jokes. Insults. Mostly us guys saying stuff to gross out the girls, so they'd come chasing us. It's amazing how easy it is to shock a girl so much that she has to chase you and hit you for it. Mixed in there were a couple fights we had to run to. Nothing good. Just some shoving and jawing. Nine out of ten fights turn out to be flops.

Then Vesto came along. In his car, of course. Slowing down to our speed, mocking us, blowing cigarette smoke at us, opening the door and tempting us to ride the rest of the way.

The girls jumped in.

When I saw Hoffman and Konski, our two defensive tackles, rush the car, I figured they were going to pull the girls out. But they didn't. They pulled Little Looie Lopezia out.

Looie is always in Vesto's car. Not because Vesto loves him so much, but because Looie has this radio, and all Vesto's dashboard has is a big, black hole where the car radio is supposed to be. So as long as Looie is along, Vesto's got sound.

So Konski and Hoffman dragged Looie and his

radio away from the car and told Vesto, "Long as you got the girls, we're keeping Looie hostage."

"Take him!" Vesto laughed and burned rubber.

Poor Looie. He wanted just to sit there and wait for Vesto to come back, but we made him walk with us. Which was bad news for him. Looie doesn't like to walk long distances with his blaster, because it's so big. Looks like a suitcase on him. As the blocks went by, the radio sank closer and closer to the ground. He tried to turn the music off — he said music made it weigh more — but we wouldn't allow that, the real hostage being the radio, not Looie. Looie's radio was as big in sound as in size. Like a portable concert. Pretty soon Looie was lugging it with both hands. Then cradling it in both arms.

That's about when Vesto showed up again. The girls hopped out of the car. Looie tried to hop back in, but he never made it. The girls wouldn't let him. They wanted to dance, and they needed the radio. They surrounded him. They closed in. They gang-snuggled him. You could see the strength coming back into Looie, the radio rising slowly from the ground. He snapped it back into one hand. He turned the volume up. He wiggled his hips. Vesto peeled away.

So we danced up the street, if you want to call it dancing. For most of us — the guys, at least — it was the first time we'd ever danced. We sure made up for lost time. It was crazy. Maybe we were drunk on radio fumes. I danced with Richie, then Calvin, then Sharon Grenauer, then Cricket Dupree, then myself. Even Peter got into the act. He picked up the front paws of a black-and-white mongrel and danced with it, crooning, "You American girls are so beeyooooo-tiful!" And suddenly there was Dugan, who wasn't even a Walker, stomping on the roof of a TV-repair van.

We were at the McDonald's then, and getting pretty hungry and thirsty, so we danced on in. Five minutes later we were downing our Big Macs and fries and McNuggets in three booths in the back. A worker told Looie to turn his radio off. Looie just turned it down, but nobody threw us out.

I was halfway through my Big Mac when Richie looked over my head toward the door and went, "Uh-oh, Herk, you're in trouble."

I turned. Marceline was coming in, heading our way, and she didn't look too happy.

"Prob'ly saw you dancing with the other girls," whispered Richie.

Great, I thought. I'd like to be in that kind of trouble. Marceline jealous — it was a new taste. I liked it.

She came back to the booths and just stood there for a minute, glaring. Not just at me, but at everybody. She wore her red button above her left breast, the one I had touched. (The rest of us had our buttons in our pockets.) Her lips were clamped tight. She was wearing her red, floppy hat. She was holding her sunglasses in one hand and a plastic binder in the other. Her lips parted, showing the little chip in her front tooth. She looked great.

"This is supposed to be a Walk for Hunger," she said. Konski pushed a fry into his mouth. A giggle came from the girls' booth. "Can't you stop stuffing yourselves long enough to finish it? Is that asking too much?"

I wanted to crawl under the table. I couldn't believe it. This was too much, even for Marceline. It's one thing not to care about your popularity, but it's something else to go out of your way, to practically beg people not to like you. This was business for some teacher or principal or parent. You don't ream out your fellow kids. Hadn't anybody ever told her that?

"It's a Walk for Hunger," said Konski, inserting another fry. "So we were hungry."

Muffled giggles.

"No rule says we can't stop," Hoffman pitched in. "We still make the same amount of money."

"Yeah, Marcy," piped Sharon Grenauer (Marceline hates to be called Marcy), "we're making the money. And we're gonna beat the other grades."

Marceline just bit her lip and glared for a while. Nobody moved. "So maybe," she finally said, "there's more to it than money and beating other grades. Maybe there's sharing. Maybe there's inconvenience. Maybe if we can inconvenience ourselves a little, maybe suffer a little, instead of riding in somebody's car or prancing around or feeding our faces, maybe we can understand just a little bit. Maybe *he* needs our understanding" — she yanked a piece of paper from the binder and threw it onto the table where I was sitting — "as much as our money." There was a red ring around each of her nostrils. She turned and walked out.

It was a picture. Of a boy. In Africa, I guess. Mostly his face. It looked kind of like a skeleton with brown skin stretched over it. His eyes were wide open, so wide it looked like his eyelids were gone. They were looking up at something above the camera. It was the flies that really got to me. They were crawling over his face, like he was a banana peel, or dead. But he wasn't. I couldn't figure it. Why wasn't he swatting them away? How could he *stand* it? Except for one time when I took off my sock and found an ant on my foot, I don't think any bug — fly, ant, mosquito, you name it — has ever landed on me and had a chance to hang around for more than one second. And yet even though it was just a still photograph, you could tell those flies had been there for a pretty good while and were going to hang around as long as they felt like it. Three of them were even pecking at the edges of his eyes, like they just moseyed on over to take a drink from those wide, white pools, like they knew he wasn't even going to blink.

The only sounds from the girls' booth behind me were eating sounds.

Peter was already heading for the door, his unfinished milk shake on the table. I folded the picture, put it in my pocket, and followed him out.

Maybe it was the food, or the dancing — I don't know — I just know we had gone only a block when I got that old fluey feeling again. While Peter waited, I whipped into Burger King and spent a long time in the men's room. Next I made it about five blocks before I had to go again, and it took another couple of agonizing blocks to find an open gas station. "You go ahead," I told Peter. He argued, but not for long. You don't argue with somebody who has to go as bad as I did. I let him give me the map before I tore for the office to ask for the bathroom key.

The big red-and-white banner was gone when I finally got back to the high school, the end of the tenth mile. Everything and everybody was gone. Except my mother.

She led me to the car. She felt my forehead. I usually push her hand away when she does that, but not this time.

"You look terrible," she said. "I told you you shouldn't have gone."

"No big deal," I said.

"Here," she said when we got in the car. She handed me an old apple juice jug filled with water. "I'll bet you haven't been drinking along the way, have you?" I didn't answer. She took off the lid and shoved the jug into my hands. "Drink."

I drank. I wondered how dehydrated I had gotten. I imagined I was like a shriveled piece of dried apple in a cereal bowl, that swells up when you pour milk over it.

I flopped into bed without changing. That night I dreamed of flies.

Bushes

Richie has a girlfriend. Cricket Dupree.

I can't believe it. Seems like just last night we were under the stands, guzzling a Miller's.

He told me it happened last Sunday, the day of the Walk. When they left McDonald's, the two of them stuck pretty much together till the end. Then, on the way home, they went into The Bushes.

I almost choked. "The Bushes!"

The Bushes are in front of the junior high, to one side of the main door. It's where you go to make out with somebody. There's a regular path through the grass to them. They're pretty high and thick, so no one can see you from the street. The Bushes are sort of the ninth-graders' motel. Or back seat.

"Yeah," he said, "stayed there till almost dark."

"Damn." I was afraid to ask, but I couldn't help myself. "What doing?"

He grinned and kind of swaggered in his seat. We were in last-period study hall. "Ate me some face, baby." He held out his hand for me to slap. I just stared at him. "I ain't kidding," he said. "She was Frenching me so bad I thought I was gonna start talking French any minute. I thought she had two tongues, she was goin' so fast." He made little darty flickers with his finger.

"You're fulla shit," I told him and went back to my algebra homework.

"You just wish it," I heard him say.

I kept working on my equations. I tried not to seem too interested, but I could feel my cheeks getting warm. "What's that s'posed to mean?"

"You figure it out."

I wished I couldn't figure it out. But I could. I knew exactly what he meant. He meant that Marceline and I weren't exactly breaking any sex records, and that he and Cricket did more in the first five minutes behind The Bushes than we had done in a year. I knew this, but I didn't want to know it. I didn't want to know it so bad that I made myself unknow it. I just kept staring at my algebra problem, and the harder I stared, the more I unknew. I unknew that he had been to The Bushes, and all of a sudden I knew that he had just been pulling my chain. Just like him, that hormone. I finished off the problem. I closed the book. I felt better.

I looked over at him. I nodded and grinned. "Right, Rich."

He turned in his seat toward me, still playing it serious. "I'm telling ya, man, I went into them Bushes, and when I came out I was in love." He doubled the last word with a growl: "luhhhhhhve."

Give him credit; he was hanging in there to the

bitter end. I gave him a thumbs-up sign, like pilots do. "Right, Rich. Go for it."

Then he was grinning and unbuttoning his shirt, his eyes drilling into me. He opened the shirt. I ripped my eyes away after half a second, no more, but it was too late. The picture was in my brain, and my brain was figuring it out and giving me the message, whether I wanted it or not. And the message was: Richie does not have three nipples. It just might look like that at first glance. One of the two side-by-side on the right — the inside one — it's not a nipple. It's a hickey.

Hickeys

Ever since I saw it, that hickey has been burning a hole in my life. It's not just Rich, either. They're showing up all over the place. You walk down the halls, and it's a parade of hickeys. Necks. Throats.

Ham has seen them too. At the community college where he teaches English. "There's a new epidemic," he said at dinner one night.

My mother handed a bowl of creamed chipped beef to set on the table. "Careful, it's hot. Epidemic of what? Who wants toast for their creamed beef?"

Everybody raised a hand but Timmy.

"Hickeys," said Ham.

"Bumps? What kind of epidemic is that?" She dropped two pieces of bread into the toaster.

"Not bumps. Hickeys."

"Hickeys *are* bumps," she said.

Ham shook his head. "Hickeys used to be bumps. But not anymore."

"What are they now?"

"Remember passion marks? Passion bites?"

"*They're* hickeys?"

"According to *Webster's Dictionary of Teenage Lexicon*, ninety-eighth revised edition."

"Well," she said, plopping a slice of white bread onto Timmy's plate and spooning some creamed beef over it, "I like them better as bumps."

"They're also called suckers," piped Cootyhead.

My mother's eyes flew open. "Do you want to go to your room?"

Cootyhead's eyes flew open even wider. "Wha'd *I* do?"

"You look around the campus," said Ham, "and you swear there's a vampire at work. Maybe an old one who's lost his teeth, so all he can do is gum your neck. Leaves marks instead of holes."

Timmy bared his fangs — "Dracula!" — and went after Cootyhead's arm.

Cootyhead smacked him.

My mother left the toaster and smacked Cootyhead on the hand with a wooden spoon. Cootyhead stared at her hand like it was going to fall off.

"That's disgusting," my mother said. The toast popped. She took out the slices and dumped them onto my plate and Cootyhead's and dropped two more slices into the toaster.

"I want toast," said Timmy.

"Too late," said my mother. "Eat that and I'll make you the next one with toast. Can't they cover it up with makeup? Or Clearasil? The girls, at least?"

Ham, still waiting for his toast, shoveled himself

some string beans. "Just the opposite. They almost go out of their way to let them show. They're badges. Girl came into my office yesterday —" He looked up, squinted, shot up from his seat, clapped his hands above his head, sat slowly back down, opened his hands, studied them. "What's a moth still doing around? It's October." He wiped one hand with his napkin. "She came into my office, to show me her outline for a paper on Coleridge, and she had them all around her neck, in a ring. I'm still not sure somebody didn't try to strangle her the night before."

Timmy reached across the table, holding his plate. He had scraped most of the creamed beef off his bread, so now it was soggy and blotched with cream. "Make toast," he said.

My mother sighed and took his plate and gave him hers. He grinned and asked her, "What's a hickey?"

"Never mind. You got your toast, now eat it."

Cootyhead laid her fork over Timmy's. "A hickey is when Jason clamps his lips on Marceline's neck and sucks as hard as he can and makes her neck all purple."

My mother pointed out of the kitchen. "Room."

Cootyhead just sat there, a smiley kind of wonder coming over her face.

My mother put her fork down. "Did you hear me?"

Everybody turned to Cootyhead. "Mom, you don't send kids to their room anymore. That's in fairy tales."

"Well, one of us is going to her room, and it sure isn't going to be me."

Cootyhead buried her head in her plate and took a bite, fighting off a laugh. She couldn't believe my mother was serious. Then Timmy grinned, "Go to *your* room, Mommy!" and a creamed-beef geyser spewed from Cootyhead's mouth. She didn't wait to be told again. The laugh vanished. She snarled and flung her fork down and jammed her chair back and got up and stomped off, grumbling all the way: "Waddaya think, sending me to my room is gonna make hickeys disappear? There's a lot worse things than hickeys going on! This is the twentieth century! People've been sucking on necks ever since the human race started! What, is every kid that ever says 'suck' gonna be sent to their room?"

Ham got up, went to the kitchen doorway. He shook his fists, he seethed with rage, he bellowed: "Get in that room and don't you *ever* come out! Your porridge will be delivered to you!" He loves this emotional stuff. He acts in amateur plays.

A door slammed upstairs.

My mother slumped. "You're a big help."

Ham sat down, his eyes scanning the ceiling. "Just doing my job."

"I'm still trying to come to terms with Jason," my mother said, blinking at me, like I was behind a plate glass window in a store, "and now she's starting up."

"Seventh grade. That's when Jason popped *his* cork."

"I just can't seem to fit things in fast enough. It seems like yesterday it was dinosaurs and dump trucks. Now all of a sudden it's beer breath and passion marks and . . . insolence. It's not that I think there shouldn't be problems. It's not so much the things. It's the tone."

"Unsavory."

"Exactly."

"Seedy."

"Mm."

"Degenerate."

"You're mocking."

Ham waved his fork. "Nope, not at all. Let's look on the bright side. Jason seems clean, hickeywise, at least."

Everybody stared at my neck. Next thing I knew, Timmy had pulled my shirt collar apart and was nosing into my throat. I shoved him away. "Nope, Dad," he said, shaking his head and frowning like a grown-up, "not a mark on him." Then he turned to me, kindly. "Don't Marceline suck your neck, Jacie?"

For a second or two, my mother sounded and looked like she was drowning. "You've eaten enough," she said. "You may leave the table."

Timmy's eyes lit up. "Do I have to go to my room?"

"I don't care where you go. Just leave the dinner table."

Timmy left the table.

"I don't think there's much to worry about as far

as Marceline is concerned," said Ham. "She's a pretty classy kid. Decidedly savory."

My mother smiled, nodded. "I like Marceline. Trouble is —" Suddenly she turned and gaped in shock. Timmy had left the table all right, but not the kitchen. He was in the doorway, his face red, his cheeks caved in, sucking for all he was worth on his own forearm.

"*Timothy!*"

Timmy vanished.

For the next minute there was only the sound of silverware and teeth meeting creamed beef and string beans.

"As I was saying —" my mother's voice was almost a whisper — "I like Marceline. And I'm sure she's good for Jason —" she stopped and looked at me, trying to find something to back up what she'd said, I guess — "although I don't like that coming out sounding as though my son is so bad off he needs a good influence."

"Let us remember," said Ham, "young Marceline is a teenager too, and therefore not without blemish. I'd guess Jason is pretty good for her too."

My mother nodded, looking at me some more, almost smiling. But puzzlement showed in her eyes. "Sometimes I wonder, though, if they're close enough to really have all that much influence over each other. One day they seem like boyfriend and girlfriend, the next day . . . I wonder."

What she wondered was whether I would satisfy her snooping by telling her exactly what the story was between Marceline and me.

I got up and left the kitchen.

Movie

Richie asked Marceline and me to go to a movie with him and Cricket.

"What's playing?" I said.

"The Dead Never Sleep."

"Where?"

"The Brookline."

"What's it about?"

"I don't know. Horror, I guess."

"Murders? Zombies? Ghosts?"

"Man," he squawked, "what do you care?"

I was just stalling, trying to think. I told him maybe, I'd have to see about it.

The next couple days I hardly thought about anything else. I knew right off that the main reason he asked us to go along was so he could do some showing off, show me how a real lover handles things. I could just picture him there, making out with Cricket, every other minute opening one eye to make sure I was catching the action — and to see how much I was getting done. Who needed it?

But then I started to look at it other ways. Like, maybe what this was was a chance. A chance to sit in the dark next to Marceline. And maybe make a move. Of course, I wouldn't say it that way to her. I'd say, "Would you like to go to a movie?" And Marceline isn't stupid. They might be the words leaving my mouth, but I bet the words going into her ears would be, "Would you like to sit next to me in the dark? And maybe give me a chance to make a move on you?" Which meant if she said yes, she would be saying yes to a bigger question than the one I asked. And if she said no . . . ?

I had to make it safer for myself. The solution turned out to be simple, a little tinkering with the question: "*Richie wants to know* if we'll go to the movies with Cricket and him."

As soon as I thought of it, I felt some of the pressure lift off. Now she couldn't think that I was just trying to nail her, because all I was doing was passing on Richie's question. And if she said no — which is what I expected — it would be like she was saying no to Rich, not me.

Sort of.

She said okay. Yes. I could hardly believe it.

When I told her what the movie was, she wrinkled her nose and asked if that was the only thing playing. I said it was, within walking distance, anyway. She looked off into the distance. I could see her brain turning the dials of the future, trying to focus in on the coming Saturday night. Finally she blinked back to the present and nodded, and that was it.

When my mother found out, she beamed and swooned: "A date!"

"It's not a date," said Ham.

She looked at him, at me. "Of course it's a date."

Ham shook his head. "May look like a date, but it's not."

She focused on me, still smiling but a little baffled too, her head tilting. "Well?"

"Well, what?"

"Isn't it a date?"

Ham answered. "Kids don't date. Not anymore."

Her head swiveled to him. "What do they do?"

"Usually they just converge. Flop into each other in some alleyway or bush, suck each other's neck for a while, then go home. Separately."

My mother digested this for a minute. She turned back to me. "Are you taking Marceline to the movies, or to an alley?"

I groaned, "Movies." I tried to escape, but she held on to my arm. I wondered if there *was* an alleyway or a bush in my near future.

"But don't call it a date," said Ham. "'Date' has the odor of antiquated corn. They are *going out*. As in, 'I am *going out* to empty the garbage.'"

"You're walking her home, aren't you?" she said.

"No. I'm shipping her Federal Express."

That gave her a good chuckle. She let me go, happy. "It's a date."

So Saturday night there we were, the four of us, heading into the lobby of the Brookline for the 7:30 showing of *The Dead Never Sleep*. Catching sight of the doorway leading to the seats made me a little nervous. I asked Marceline if she wanted some candy. She said no.

"Popcorn?"

"No."

"Soda?"

"Nope."

"Nothing? I'm buying, y'know."

She stuck her hand out. "I'll take the cash."

I went to the counter myself and got popcorn. The jumbo size. A bucket. Buttered. Richie and Cricket were hanging at the doorway, scowling at me, itchy, like lions at feeding time. After getting my popcorn, I went over to check out the soda machine.

"Herkimer!" Richie growled.

I handed the popcorn to Marceline and pulled up to the water fountain. The Brookline water fountain is one of those ancient jobs, like an old sink. No cooler. I let the water run for a minute, and it was still warm.

"Herkimer!"

I drank a little and took back the popcorn. "Damn water's like bathwater," I complained, but Richie and Cricket weren't there to listen. They were already going in. They went down about halfway and turned left, to the side section. Cricket went in first, but as soon as they sat down, they got right back up again and traded places. I wondered if it had anything to do with Richie being left-handed. So the way that left the seating was: me — Marceline — Cricket — Richie.

Right off the bat, that made me a little uncomfortable, because Marceline and Cricket were not exactly bosom buddies. Not that they hated each other; they just didn't have much in common — Cricket the cheerleader, Marceline the tromboner. Marceline is funny about cheerleaders. She says you couldn't pay her enough to be one. (Not that anybody was asking her to.) But as I see it, the thing about cheerleaders is, if you *can* be one, you *want* to be one. And if you can't be one, you wish you could, or dream about it. Who ever heard of a girl who wouldn't be a cheerleader if she had the chance? It would be like a beauty pageant girl saying, "Nah, here, take this crown back. I don't want to be Miss America." Well, I guess there's one person who would turn them both down, cheerleader — even captain! — and Miss America. Marceline McAllister. Bet on it.

Richie and Cricket didn't waste any time. Before the main feature, before the short subject, before the lights went out — or even down — they were going at it.

Now, there's a kind of etiquette for times like this. It's not written down anywhere, but everybody seems to know it. You better, because there's no telling when or where you're going to bump into somebody making out. I mean, it's more than alleyways and bushes. Anytime you turn a corner, come down a stairway, open a door, cross a street — it could happen. The point is, when it happens to you, everything's cool. You act like you don't see them. No big deal. It's the code. Common courtesy.

So what does Marceline do? Richie and Cricket

go into their clinch, and Marceline jerks her head toward them, like a Martian has just sat down next to her. And does she turn away, a little embarrassed at herself? Noooo. She keeps gawking at them, at the same time leaning away, toward me, like she's afraid they might explode any second.

Finally she settled back in her seat and turned to me. "I was all set to have a nice conversation." She made a pouting face, but her eyes were grinning.

I whispered. "Maybe they just want to squeeze in a little get-acquainted time before the movie starts."

"Shall I offer them some popcorn?" She was whispering, but loud.

"I don't think they want any."

She took another long gawk at them. I was ready to crack up. "Guess you're right." She scooped out a handful of popcorn for herself.

Well, of course, the lovers didn't let up. The lights went out, the short subject (an exciting look at the fascinating world of patchwork quilting) came and went, and then the dead who never slept came oozing up out of their tombs.

By now I was pretty tense. The moment was here. The movie. The girl. The dark. I could practically feel the soft, fuzzy seat nudging me toward her, practically hear it hissing: Make your move now . . . now. *But what move?* I used to think that by the time you got to ninth grade, your moves just naturally showed up, on schedule, like hair and hormones and knowing how to change a tire. But then came the babysitting bungle, and I realized that if I was ever going to have moves, I would have to build them from the ground up, like muscles.

That's when I started fantasizing. And I started fantasizing because I remembered seeing a high jumper on TV once, and he just stood in front of the bar in a trance for five minutes, twitching and shaking his arms and legs. The announcer said he was doing the jump, every step, every movement of it, in his head, and he wouldn't start the real jump until he saw himself clear the bar in his head. Mind over matter, the announcer said.

So I started trying it. I pictured myself making moves — big moves, little moves, cool moves, killer moves. The moves were just rolling off me, and everywhere girls were swooning, hanging limp, their eyes closed, their faces drifting closer and closer to mine, their lips parting. Sometimes they swooned as soon as they saw me coming, before I even went into a warm-up move — they knew it was useless to resist.

Then there was the greatest move of all. The ultimate. Trouble was, I could never get the picture to come in crystal-clear, could never see exactly what I was doing or hear exactly what I was saying. But it was there, just a knob-turn away, I sensed it. I called it my Star Trek Move: . . . *to go boldly where no move has ever gone before.*

Cheerleaders, captains, prom queens, drum majorettes, fast-food waitresses — in my fantasies they all swooned under my moves . . . but I was sitting next to Marceline McAllister. And plopped down right behind us, like a jury sent to judge me, were four adults.

As if all that wasn't bad enough, Marceline complicated things even more by refusing to shut up. The reason the dead on the screen couldn't sleep was because these high-school kids kept going out to their cemetery and raising hell: knocking over gravestones, banging on the tomb doors, howling like ghosts, turfing the grass. The dead had some pretty neat ways of getting back at the kids, and no scene could get by without Marceline poking me and whispering her little comment: "Was that supposed to *scare* me? . . . I've been more scared going down to my own *cellar* . . . *Now* I know why I never come to see this kind of stinkola . . . This isn't scary, it's *funny* . . . I'm supposed to be *believing* this. Why aren't I *believing* it? . . . Because it's *stupid* . . . Who made this dung ball? . . . If the dead want to sleep, all they have to do is watch this movie!"

And when she wasn't reviewing the movie, she was reviewing the Richie and Cricket Show: "Pssst — Jason — this is better than the movie . . . More scary, anyway . . . It's getting noisy over there. Can you hear? . . . Should I offer them some popcorn? . . . Pssst — Jason — *look!*"

I knew she was being funny — whether or not she was trying to be was another question — but I was under too much pressure to work up a good laugh. I was being bombarded by three performances — the movie, Richie and Cricket, and Marceline — but all I could think about was getting my own performance started. And when Marceline poked me and said, "Is *that* why you brought me here?" I went so stiff you could have hoisted me out of there like a manikin.

Then Richie was getting up and edging for the aisle. "Gotta go wee-wee," he said. Cricket giggled. As he passed me he gave me a quick, sharp knuckle in the arm. I knew what the message was: *Do something*.

I thought it would be kind of awkward, the three of us alone, Marceline and Cricket next to each other, and it was. For Cricket. Before Richie hit the aisle, Marceline was all over her: "Isn't this movie great . . . Oh man, you don't know what you're missing . . . When that guy was sleeping, do you *believe* what crawled up his nose? . . . Do you think it was trick photography? . . . Maybe it was a stunt-man . . . a stunt *nose!*"

Poor Cricket didn't know which side was up. I got a sore stomach holding in the laughs.

Mercifully, Richie came back, knuckling my arm again as he slipped past me. Thirty seconds later Marceline was shaking me. "They're in the same seat!"

I tried to look without being too obvious. She was right. They were both in Cricket's seat. In the dim light, they could have been mistaken for one large

person. The adults behind us were nudging each
other and nodding. And shhhh-ing, because Marceline kept talking and talking. She wouldn't quit. She
had always been a pretty good talker, but I had
never seen her like this.

Then I reached into the jumbo bucket, felt all
around, and came up with nothing but butter on my
fingertips. That's when I got my second message of
the night. It wasn't as clear as Richie's, and it was
jammed full of maybes. It had to do with Marceline
gobbling up all the popcorn and jabbering every second of the way, and it came to a ram-shocker of a
conclusion: *Maybe — maybe — she's as nervous as
I am.*

Face

Maybe . . .

Was it enough to go on?

I got up, went to the men's room, got a drink of warm water, loitered around the candy case, came back. If anything, Marceline talked even more. Faster. Like she had to catch me up on everything I'd missed.

I took her hand. Held it. The rush of words stopped. She stiffened. Her eyes shot over to mine. ("Is *that* why you brought me here?") She turned away. The light from the screen caught her eyes. I thought of an animal's eyes frozen in the headlights of our car. She seemed to relax. I was careful not to hold her hand too tight, so she could pull out if she wanted.

She didn't.

But she did keep talking. Blah-blah-blah. I tried to detect if any of the hand pressure was coming from her, or was I doing all the holding? I couldn't be sure. I experimented. I loosened my grip a little — a little more — to see if she would pick up the slack. She did — her fingers tightened, just a hair, on mine. Then they went limp again, our hands flopped apart. I quick grabbed her again, held on this time. Blah-blah-blah.

Blah-blah-blah-blah-blah-blah-blah-blah-blah . . .

Up on the screen, one of the dead was slipping under the sheets of a sleeping kid. I shifted sideways in my seat (Blah-blah-blah), till I was facing her and, just beyond her nose, the dark form of the Two That Became One. I kept hold of her hand with my left (Blah-blah-blah) and swung my right arm around, across her front, and closed my fingers (Blah-blah-blah) around her upper arm. I felt her go tense. "Shut up," I whispered. Unbelievably (Bl—), she shut up. But her eyes were still on the screen, straight ahead, unblinking, wide (two little screens meeting one big screen), like she had suddenly discovered this was the greatest movie she had ever seen. I leaned forward, bringing my face — my self — close to her, closer, closer . . . Crazily, I thought about astronauts trying to dock their ship with another module in space — how hard it is, a thousand times trickier than it looks, because the two ships are moving at different speeds in different orbits. Well, I've got news for the astronauts: docking two spacecraft is nothing compared to trying to kiss Marceline McAllister. (And she wasn't even moving!) It was taking me light-years — light-lifetimes — to travel the inches between us. In the movie-screen gleam of her wide-open eyes I saw the faces of the other two girls I had kissed — Missy Cuyler at Mark Wiggans's birthday party, and Heather Newsome behind the Dumpster at 7-Eleven. Those times had been easy. Nothing for me to do. The girls grabbed me.

As I came closer to Marceline, the reflected light went out in her right eye, then her left, as the shadow of my face passed over hers. (A total eclipse!) The eyes of the adults behind us were gleaming, gleaming out of faces I would never know, pale and ghostly faces, watching, watching . . . and then I saw nothing, because my own eyes were shut. (Toss a baby into the water and it holds its breath: kiss a girl and your eyelids come down.) And then, at long long last, the only spot possible in all the universe — a little jolt, a bump, too hard — throttle back, ease off — there, okay, okay ("Mission Control — We have contact!") — as perfect a landing as I was ever going to make.

Her head went back — was I pushing her or kissing her? — back, back, then down a little too — was she trying to slip out from under me? Then she stopped. Her head was resting against the back of the seat. She took three or four quick breaths, then a long one, then regular. Her arm relaxed in my hand. Then I felt movement in her arm — it was rising. Then something touching me, lightly — her hand was on my shoulder. Was she going to push me away? . . . No. The hand was just resting there, staying there, lightly.

We pulled back from each other, about an inch. "Hey —" she said. I waited for more, but that was all. "Hey —" She sounded kind of groggy. Her eyes were closed. I closed my eyes, and in our butter-smelling blindnesses we located each other again. This time I felt a little pressure coming from her lips, and the touch of her hand on my shoulder became more than a touch.

Then, suddenly, the lights were on. We pulled apart, but not as far apart as we had been before we kissed. It seemed we had just started five seconds before. From the corner of my eye I could see that the Two That Became One were becoming two again, like an amoeba splitting. The people behind us were already heading up the aisle.

Believe it: no time flies like kissing time.

Us

I am floating.

Leaves fall like fire flakes from flaming trees. Ham brought the last of his tomatoes in — green — and put them in brown paper bags in the cellar. I hear squabbling dogs in the distance, and a minute later I look up to see necklaces of geese sailing across a mashed-potato sky. Darkness creeps closer and closer to dinnertime. They say it's going to be the coldest winter in years. I don't care.

I am warm. Floating. Warm.

Richie says, "Took you long enough to get started."

I just grin, remembering.

I remember a lot. During class. In bed. Eating. It's kind of like viewing a videotape. I rewind back through time, jog down to the right hour, the right minute, the right instant, when it started, the true beginning of it, not the first touch of the first kiss, but the moment when it hit me that maybe she was nervous too. Then I run the tape forward, at whatever speed I want. Usually slow-forward. If something took one second in the movie seats, I can stretch it out to ten seconds. Or sixty.

My personal replay gives me more than any regular videotape, more than just pictures and sounds. It gives me touch and feel and smell and softness and closeness. And something that doesn't have a word for it. It's a little like the feeling you get when you're tearing halfway between second and third base and all of a sudden you realize you're not going to stop at third because they're just catching up with the ball, so you're going to make your turn at third and try for a home run.

Or like turning over a flat rock down by the creek and instead of finding the usual dull-brown salamander, you're looking at a glossy black-and-yellow striped job that's so neat it makes you ache and you almost want to cry.

Or like coming in from the snow to a steaming mug of hot chocolate.

Or a little like all of those things put together.

Only better.

A zillion times better.

I have everything I want. If there's something I don't have, that's okay, because I don't want it anyway.

I take that back. There is one thing I want. I want to stop every person I see — kids, teachers, janitors — and tell them. Especially my mother.

I see Marceline, and it's different now. There's something new. Before, there was a She and there was a Me. Now there is an Us. And when we separate to go to our homerooms or different classes or our homes, the Us is still there. The Us is secret and sure and always.

I sleep, and sometimes she is there too. And sometimes when I open my eyes I have a feeling that something woke me up, a voice. And then I hear it, the last faint echo of it as it swirls down the sinkhole of my sleep: "Hey —"

It

The Stairwell.

Richie's mouth was all grin, but his eyes were information. "D'juh hear?"

"What?"

"Kupchak and Breen."

Harry Kupchak. Debbie Breen. Ninth-graders. They were going together.

"What about 'em?"

"They did it."

"Did what?" He just kept grinning. He didn't answer. Didn't have to. "*Yeah?*"

Ripley answered, "Yeah."

"When?" said Morgan.

"Last night," said Peale.

"Where?" said Pinto.

"Her house," said Wallach.

"Babysitting," said Flagg.

"Her basement," said Chilbano.

"Damn," said Bortner.

"Go, Kupchak," said Dunn.

Strange day. Strange atmosphere. You went to

your usual classes — Algebra, English, Science —
but there was really only one subject, and one text-
book: *Doing It* by Kupchak and Breen. The radiators
hissed, the water fountains gurgled: *They did
it . . . They did it . . .*

When Harry Kupchak and Debbie Breen came
hand-in-hand into the cafeteria, nobody had to tell
you. You knew. They sat at a table along the
inside wall, and you could almost feel the whole
floor tilt in their direction. They sat on the same
side of the table. Close. Smiling. Looking. Talking
a little. Not eating much. Nobody sat with them. You
couldn't really catch anyone staring at them,
but if one of them had picked up a dollar from the
floor, three hundred kids would have checked their
pockets.

It was during lunch when Richie started his attack. "Looks like Kupchak beat you to it. I thought
all this time she was saving it for you."

He was referring to the fact that I used to like
Debbie Breen. She was a cheerleader. Blond. We
had a little thing going there for a while. Nothing
serious. Hayrides, stuff like that. What the heck,
we were only in seventh grade. After a while I moved
on to Marceline. She still is a cheerleader. Debbie
is. Captain now.

"Man, stop busting my bunions," I told him.

"You know you'd like to be Kupchak."

I cut up my sloppy joe. "Where'd you get your crystal ball?"

"You *know* it."

Peter and Calvin came over, sat down.

"I'll tell you what I know. I know I already got a chick, so I don't need Debbie Breen, or anybody else."

Peter's eyes bulged. "You're raising chickens?"

Peter Kim—type humor, which has been plaguing us lately. Even though Peter is one hundred percent American, born in the U.S.A., he thinks it's funny to pretend he just stepped off the plane from Korea and doesn't understand Yankee ways.

"Peter," I said, "your mother."

Peter frowned, then brightened. "Your grandmother!"

Groans all around.

"Just think, Herk," said Rich, "you could've been him. If you'da hung in there."

"Who says I want to be him? Who says I ain't doing okay being me?"

His grin was red and meaty with sloppy joe. "Tell me you wouldn't trade McAllister for Breen."

I felt like stuffing his sloppy joe up his nose. "I'm telling ya."

He burst out laughing; a sloppy-joe pellet sailed past my ear. "Riiiight, big lover!"

"Why don't you ask me if I'd trade her for that airhead you're going with?"

Another laugh-bomb. "Sorry, Herk ol' boy, I know just how much you've got the hots for Cricket, but she belongs to this dude. All of her, if you know what I mean."

"Half of Marceline is worth all of that worm-brain."

He roared. There was no touching him. "Bet your half," he sputtered, "doesn't include something nice and soft, 'bout the size of an orange —" He put his hand out, fingers curling up, like he was squeezing the orange.

I thought of the babysitting, the Scrabble game, reaching across the board . . . right then I could feel her breast in my hand, kind of like a water balloon. "Maybe I just don't talk about it."

"Maybe you just don't have anything to talk *about*."

"Maybe there's no point in saying anything once you've been in your girlfriend's bedroom, because hormonal deficiencies like you wouldn't understand what I'm talking about anyway."

The grin still held its ground, but his eyes took a step backward. He shut up. I had reached him.

Nobody said anything for a while. The four of us just munched away on our sloppy joes. Richie kept wagging his head with a smacked-ass kind of grin. I knew he didn't want to believe me. He was scrounging around for a reason not to. But he was stuck, a worm on a hook, because he knew that I wouldn't say something like that about Marceline unless it was true.

Finally Calvin said, looking straight at me, into me, "Why don't you guys, uh, come over to my house after school."

Reproduction

I was amazed at how much Calvin's room had changed since I'd seen it last. It looked like a combination laboratory and doctor's office. Only the bed gave it away as a bedroom.

Charts, books, bones were everywhere. But what kept us busy — and speechless for the first five minutes — was a bookcase with no books. Instead, there were jars, dozens of them. They were capped and filled with a clear liquid, and each jar had something floating in it. About half of them were insects and worms. Bees, wasps, roaches, beetles, thousand-leggers — some of those suckers I'm glad I'd never run into. A horsefly big enough to saddle. Humongousest bloodworm I've ever seen, bigger than the garter snake in the jar next to it. Then there was the other stuff. Parts. I thought I recognized one, at least.

"Chicken heart?" I said.

Calvin nodded.

I tried the next one. "Big, *big* chicken heart."

"Turkey heart."

From then on I just pointed and Calvin identified.

"Gizzard, chicken . . . gizzard, turkey . . . liver, turkey . . . kidney, lamb . . . heart, steer . . . thymus gland, calf . . . stomach, cow . . ."

That was enough. "Calvin, what are you, some kind of ghoul?" He just glared at me, huffy, and sniffed, sort of like Marceline does. "Really, Cal, where'd you get this stuff?"

"Supermarket."

"Get out."

"True. Some of those, I got them just as my mother was going to cut them up for gravy. I told her I wanted to practice surgery on them. So now every once in a while she brings me home something."

"Yeah, but a *kidney?* Nobody's gonna eat a kidney."

"People do."

"They're full of piss."

"That's the bladder."

"So what's the kidney do?"

"It makes the urine and sends it to the bladder."

Peter chimed in: "I thought the balls did that." He went to a huge chart, almost as tall as himself, hanging on the closet door. It showed a naked man. Well, not naked, really — skinned — so you could see everything inside. Peter pointed to the bean-shaped organs in the chart-man's lower back. "The balls."

"Wrong," said Calvin. "The kidneys."

"Well, yeah," said Peter, "that's their real name. But you also call them the balls, right?"

"Nope," said Calvin, his face as serious as Peter's. "They're just kidneys." He had no idea Peter was pulling his chain.

Peter shook his head, frowning. "I don't think so."

"You don't think what?" Calvin huffed.

"I don't think they're just kidneys."

"Peter, it doesn't have anything to do with what you *think*, or what *I* think. That's just the way it *is*. A kidney is a kidney. Period."

"In Korea a kidney is a ball."

"Fine. Great."

"In Korea, if you tell a doctor your balls hurt, he tells you to take off your shirt."

"Great."

Calvin was looking out his window, his arms folded. Richie and I were gagging.

"So," said Peter, all innocent, "do Americans have balls?"

Calvin just stood still for another thirty seconds. Then he turned, took a pencil from his desk, and gave two hard raps to the chart-man, between the legs. Peter wagged his head again, slowly, painfully, like he really hated having to do this to Calvin. Calvin rapped the chart again. "Testicles! Balls!"

Peter shrugged, sighed, shook his head. "Kumquats."

Three minutes later we were still laughing so hard that Mrs. Lemaine had to knock against the kitchen ceiling to make us quiet down. Even Doctor C had to crack a smile.

"So," said Richie, his face still red, "what are you gonna do? Give Herkimer a vasectomy?"

I stared at him. What was he getting at? "What's that?" I said.

"It's when you get spaded," explained Richie. "Like they do to cats. Only now they do it to people too."

"*What* do they do?"

"Chop your balls off. Or some part of them, anyway."

Peter cupped his gonads. "You people are barbarians!"

"What the hell *for?*" I said.

"So you won't have any more kids," answered Richie. "My father had it done to him."

"No wonder," said Peter.

Now I was getting it. And now I was getting an idea why Calvin had wanted me here. A little birds-and-bees lesson. And now was my chance to clear up what I had said in the cafeteria. My chance to say, Hey, listen, it's true I was in her bedroom, but I never said we *did* anything.

My chance . . .

Calvin held up his hand. "Nothing gets chopped off. You make a little incision and cut the vas deferens, that's all. Look."

He pulled out from under his bed something that looked like the world's biggest notepad, about the size of the top of a school desk. He laid it on the bed and started flipping the pages. They were drawings of body parts. He stopped when he came to the page titled "Male Reproductive System." It was real detailed, even showed hair follicles. There were wavy things and squiggly things going all over the place. All in different colors. And each with its own name. More names than you see on a map of the moon. There's more to a ball than meets the eye. And you could see on the drawing something that I myself had noticed even before I got to first grade: they're shaped more like eggs than balls. Why don't they call them eggs? ("That guy's got brass eggs.")

"Here's where you do it." Calvin was pointing with the pencil. "Snip it here, then over here. Cauterize. Sew them up. Takes fifteen minutes."

"Thanks anyway," I said.

Richie started flipping through the chart book, till he came to "Female Reproductive System." He stopped dead and whistled faintly through his front teeth. The rest of us stood staring. I mean, it wasn't exactly *Playboy* or *Penthouse;* it was just a drawing like all the others, official and medical and labeled, but still . . .

Calvin was tracing the route a sperm cell has to take to get to an egg. "They start here, millions of them . . . around here . . . up this way . . . over here . . . out through here . . . now it really starts getting rough . . . through here . . . this way . . . lots of them drop off here . . . down to thousands now . . . through here . . . here . . . finally, *here* . . . maybe only a hundred now . . . trying to get in . . . only one will."

"Like salmon swimming upstream," said Peter.

It was exhausting just to hear about it. In real bodies, the route is only a couple inches long, but on the chart it looked like going from New York to Los Angeles. And that's just about how far it is from the sperm's point of view, Calvin said, since they're so miniscule.

". . . and here they are trying to fertilize the egg."

Calvin had flipped the page, and now we were looking at a close-up of sperms ganging up on an egg. One thing jumped out at me right off the bat: the size of the egg. It was huge. Titanic. Even though there was a whole mob of sperms, they looked like pushovers for the egg, because it was so much bigger than all the sperms put together. Like a basketball being attacked by ants.

"Doesn't seem fair," Peter said.

We all looked at him, wondering what the joke was now. He was looking down at the chart, expression serious as usual.

"What do you mean?" I said.

He shrugged. "Oh, all that trouble they go to, all excited like, looking forward . . . then some kind of birth control bumps them off. Or when they get there, *it's* not there. Like —" he pretended to be a stood-up sperm — "Hey, where's the egg?"

"If you don't," said Calvin, his eyes sliding toward me, "you wind up with a baby."

"The girl winds up," said Rich.

"Everybody winds up," said Calvin.

We watched as his pencil point traced the final route of the final sperm, the only one that would make it all the way, that would wriggle its way into the egg, a comet invading the sun.

Suddenly Mrs. Lemaine was in the doorway (Red Alert! Female among the sperms!), just long enough to smile and say, "Calvin, I hate to break this up, but dinner is in five minutes."

We trooped downstairs. Calvin pulled me over by the piano, whispered. "Be careful, okay?"

"Oh, yeah," I said. "No sweat."

Why wasn't I saying it? *Calvin, about that bedroom stuff* . . .

"Careful."

"Yeah. Careful."

"I have some more stuff I can show you."

"Yeah, I'll check it out later. Gotta go, Doc. Seeya."

Gametes

Since that day in Calvin's room, I've been thinking a lot about gametes. That's the official name for sex cells. Sperms and eggs.

Sperms are funny little suckers. I can't decide exactly how I feel about them.

At first I wasn't too crazy about them. Especially when I saw a sperm's size compared to an egg's. I mean, guys are supposed to be bigger than girls, right? (Myself, I'm a slow-grower. I'll probably be six foot by the time I'm eighteen.) So it seems kind of upside down that sperms should be so puny and eggs so huge. I can't help thinking that whenever I have to look up at a girl, it would be a nice consolation to know that my sperm is bigger than her egg.

Calvin says it's dumb to feel that way, because all us males are in the same boat. We might all be different sizes on the outside, but if you lined everybody's sperms up side by side, you wouldn't be able to tell the difference between them.

"You mean," I said, "my sperms are just as big as Hulk Hogan's?"

Calvin nodded. "As big as Andre the Giant's."

Finding that out made my day. Or at least my minute.

Anyway, let the girls have it size-wise, because when it comes to numbers, it's guys all the way. Calvin says a girl only produces one egg a month. That surprises me. Chickens turn out one a day, don't they? Yet with sperms, you're talking millions. In less time than it takes a girl to manufacture one egg, says Calvin, a guy — even a fourteen-year-old kid — can knock off a *billion* sperms. At any given moment — right now, for instance — says Calvin, there's maybe a hundred million sperms swinging down there in one gonad. Double that to get the total — two hundred million.

And the amazing thing is, every one of them is like a tiny, tiny me. Or a blueprint of me, as Calvin says. It's the genes and chromosomes and stuff. They contain all the instructions on how to make a me, a Jason M. Herkimer, and not a Richie Bell or a Dugan or a sea elephant. And the instructions cover everything. Inside each of those little tadpoles is an order saying, "Make his eyes brown." And, "Make his fingers this long and his nose that long. . . . Make this kid good at picking up ground balls. . . . Give him a one-note singing voice . . . and no hair under his arms till just before ninth grade . . ." Two hundred million tiny, identical, perfect me's. Awesome.

But I guess the thing I like best of all about sperms is their grit. There's no such thing as a wimp sperm. They might be puny-looking, but every one's a stand-up dude. Going for it all . . . The Egg or Bust! . . . pushing on, pushing on . . . dropping by the thousands . . . millions. It's a regular Bataan Death March in there. Worse, actually, because only one survives, one makes it all the way. The rest bust a gut and die trying. They all give everything they have. It's just that the winner had a little more to give.

It's nature's way, says Calvin. Only the strongest and the best make it to the egg, and only the best of the best, the champ sperm, gets inside the egg. So figure, nine months before I was born, I was already one in two hundred million.

As for the egg — I don't know — it's hard to get a fix on it. Sometimes it has a little hint of Humpty Dumpty. Or a Happy Face. Or Jabba the Hutt. But most of the time it doesn't seem to have anything going for it at all. It's just . . . there. But then, when you're that big, I guess that's all you have to be.

If I had to say one word about the egg, I guess I would say "snooty." Sitting back there. Arms folded. No sweat. Playing hard to get. Daring the little squigglers to try to get in.

One full-moon night I looked up at the sky, and just for a second or two I had the weirdest idea that it wasn't a moon and stars I was looking at, but some awesome reproductive system — sperm-stars raining down on the egg-moon from all points of the universe. So far the stars weren't having much luck, but they still had a long, long time to try.

Seconds

We all went out on Halloween. Together. For the last time. We didn't wear costumes, we were past that. Except Calvin. He couldn't stand giving it all up. He went as a Ruptured Appendix.

After eight o'clock we had the streets pretty much to ourselves. Most of the little goblins and ghoulies were back home. The people who came to the doors weren't too crazy about us. You could tell they thought they were done giving out stuff for the night; then along came these teenage jokers, invading the little kids' territory. Disgraceful. That's when the Ruptured Appendix came in handy. He would step out from behind the rest of us, and all of a sudden the person would drop the scowl — looking one-third amused, one-third confused, and one-third sick — ask Calvin "what in the world" he was supposed to be, and reach for the goodies.

Speaking of goodies, we bumped into Jewel Fiorito and some other girls making the rounds. Jewel was wearing a long coat. Her friends started tugging at it and giggling and telling her to show us guys her costume. She looked embarrassed. When two of the girls managed to pull the coat off her, eyes started popping — she was dressed as a belly dancer.

Jewel said it wasn't just a costume, she really did take belly-dancing classes. Richie grabbed her coat from one of the girls. "Okay," he grinned, "you get your coat back as soon as we get a demonstration."

She kept saying she didn't want to, but nobody believed her. When she saw Richie wasn't kidding, she sighed and said, "I need the castanets." Richie fished them out of her coat pockets, handed them to her, and the dance was on.

She made that stomach of hers do everything but lace up sneakers. Her bellybutton went in circles, first clockwise, then counterclockwise, then in and out, in and out, like a goldfish mouth, and then it was going in circles *and* in and out at the same time. Meanwhile, the castanets were knocking like horse hooves coming down the street, and the tinselly strips of her shimmering costume were doing their own dance all over her body. I think it's the closest I ever came to being hypnotized.

All of a sudden she lunged toward Richie, snatched her coat away, put it on, and clacked a castanet in his face. "Show's over."

The girls took off, and we all hauled our pillowcases back to Richie's kitchen to check out our loot and make trades.

Richie was busy chucking spiced wafers, which he hates, into the community pile, which anyone could pick from. "How'd you like to plunk your face between *them* babies?" He was gritting his teeth. Nobody had to ask him what he was talking about.

I was surprised. I was used to Richie talking that way before — most of us did — but since he was going with Cricket now ("I'm in luhhhhhhve!"), was it okay? Could you be in love with one girl and want to stick your face into another's chest? I had never had a serious thought about Cricket before, but now I did. I wondered how she would feel if she knew.

Dugan chucked a dwarf box of raisins onto the pile. "I could handle it."

Rich Frisbeed a spiced wafer into Peter's chest. "Well, P.K.? Could you handle it?"

Peter examined the wafer and dropped it into his sack. "My whole face? I don't know . . ." He looked stumped. "How about just my nose?"

I joined the others in laughing at Peter, but for me it was a nervous laugh. I had a problem: what should my answer be? The main cause of the problem was something that, when I first thought about it, amazed even me: I didn't *want* to put my face between Jewel Fiorito's knockers. A couple weeks before, I guess I would have, but since then there was The Kiss, and The Kiss was blotting out everything else. I mean, I enjoyed watching Jewel do her dance and all; but that's all it was for me — watching — she never got farther than my eyeballs. I didn't have any feelings about her. I didn't feel like I wanted to touch her, be in a movie with her, do stuff with her. I had Marceline. I was a happy dude.

But I couldn't say that. ("Hey, d'juh hear about Herkimer? Said he wouldn't even go *near* Jewel's jugs!") Talk about laughingstock! I'd have to turn in my membership as a Ninth-Grade Boy. Even Peter hadn't given a flat-out no. And Calvin was fumbling out something about maybe, in the interest of medicine, just to check for lumps . . .

Eyes were swinging toward me.

"So, Herk?"

I had to stall. I grabbed a cookie, Bugs-Bunnied it. "Ahhh — what's da question, doc?"

The real question was, why was this such a problem for me in the first place? And why wasn't it a problem for Rich? Obviously, he had worked it out. Somehow. I believed him when he said he loved Cricket. He was crazy about her, no question. Why else would he buy her a gold ankle chain? And yet, here he was, saying — growling — that he'd like to nuzzle into Jewel's jalopies, and I believed *that* too. They were both true. It was some kind of juggling act, keeping two things in the air at once. How did he do it? On the other hand, how could I not do it? How could any self-respecting American male *not* want to plunk his face between them babies? What was the matter with me?

"You're stalling, Herk."

Suddenly, like a gift from outer space, the answer was there, in my head, the answer that would let me have it both ways. "Forget it," I said, showing them a sneer. "I'm not interested in Vesto's sloppy seconds."

I could feel the pressure fall off me.

Richie shrieked. "Seconds? You mean *twenty-*seconds!"

"Get out," I said.

"Man, where you been? You think Vesto's been the only one getting a handful all this time?"

"He ain't?" Actually, I knew about all this, but I kept saying stuff to keep him aimed away from me. "Who else?"

Richie went down the list. Then Dugan added some, one of them from Holy Ghost. Calvin didn't have any to add. Neither did Peter. He wasn't joking anymore. He looked kind of glum.

It seemed like every ninth-grader in town — except the five of us around the kitchen table — had had a shot at Jewel Fiorito. Especially amazing when you stop to think that as an eighth-grader she was nobody. I thought of all those hands that had been on those babies. The picture in my mind showed them all at once — hands, everywhere, reaching in, covering her, hands two and three deep, digging, squirming, snuffling, trying to get in — like puppies, a litter, a humongous litter of hands.

"Think she does it?" I said.

Richie's head shot back, like a snake ready to strike. Everything from his mouth to his eyebrows came screwed together in the middle of his face, like, What planet did *you* come from? "No," he sneered finally, "and beans don't make you fart."

"Just wondering," I said.

The fact was, this *was* news to me, about Jewel doing the Big I.T. All this time, I kept thinking the action never went below her mammaries.

"Ever talk to Lucas?" said Rich.

"Nope."

"Ask him what happened when he had her in the dugout at the Legion field. Ever talk to Wysocki?"

"Nope."

"Bubble-gum factory parking lot. Jenks?"

"Nope."

"Art supply closet."

"Art supply closet!"

He wagged his head in amazement. "Well, there ya go. That's what happens when you stop going to The Stairwell. You don't learn nothing."

True. Since The Kiss, I had walked Marceline to school every day. And stayed with her till second bell rang. I was glad Richie had pointed this out. I liked the way nobody made a big deal out of it. Like, that's just how it is: Herkimer and McAllister. It made me feel even closer to Marceline.

On the way home I kept feeling better and better.

I could see now that I had been put through a test — tempted by the jiggling jugs — but I didn't cave in. I passed. I stuck by her. By Us. I was loyal. Yeah, that's what I was.

Kiss

A kiss isn't over when it's over. I mean, you pull your lips apart and you stand up and you walk away to different houses, maybe miles away from each other, but the kiss kind of keeps on going. You can feel it. Hours afterward. The next morning. Days afterward. Reminds me of an old Tootsie Roll commercial I saw: "It's lasting through the chase scene! . . . It's lasting through the fight scene!! . . . It's laaaasting through the love scene!!!"

That's how it was with me. The Kiss lasted through the big news on Kupchak and Breen and through the sex lessons at Calvin's and through Halloween. It lasted for almost a week. During that time, all I had to do was close my eyes, and I was back at the movie. With her. I could even smell the popcorn.

The best time was morning. I don't know if it has a name, but there's a special couple seconds of time between the end of sleep and start of being awake — it's like when you're climbing up out of the bathtub but part of you is still in the nice, warm water — that's when. I'd be climbing up out of my warm sleep-bath, and there it was, waiting for me. The Kiss. And since I wasn't totally awake, I didn't know at first that that's what it was. And for the first split micro-instant, it would seem like I had sleepwalked into something, like maybe someone was holding a piece of fruit to my lips, a peach maybe; but long before my lip sensors could send a "Bite" message to my brain, I knew this was no peach — this was better than the sweetest crushed mouthful of grapes there ever was, and it was filling up some second stomach I never knew I had.

On the Friday after the movies — six days later — Marceline had band practice after school. She didn't know I was waiting till she came out, lugging her case and her books and gabbing with the other tromboners, who are all boys. When she saw me, her eyes lit up; she said "Seeya" to the others and headed straight for me.

"Hi," she said.

"Hi."

"What're you doing here?"

"Oh, waiting for somebody."

"Anybody I know?"

Hoots came from the band passing in the background. A tuba farted, people laughed. I loved it. I loved having everybody watch us, having Us be the center of attention.

"Could be," I grinned. "You know that foxy clarinet player?"

She kicked me, but her eyes were still sparkling. "Just for that —" She shoved her trombone case into my arms.

Now I had my own books plus my gym stuff plus her case to carry, but that was okay with me. I had never carried any of her stuff before. It had occurred to me a couple times, but I was afraid to ask. I was afraid of how she'd react. If there's one thing Marceline isn't, it's helpless. And I guess I'm not exactly the Sir Galahad type.

So we went tromping out of school together. After a couple blocks, one of my sneaker laces came undone and started flap-flopping all over the place. I didn't think too much of it, but for Marceline it was a different story. She hates untied laces, and this one was a champ: *flap-flop, flap-flop*.

Finally, in front of the Methodist church, she had had enough. She stopped and glared down at my foot. I groaned. "You're not gonna make me put all this stuff down just to tie a shoelace, are you?"

She was debating. Her arms were loaded too, with a ton of books. Her eyes came up from my foot to my face, to my eyes, and next thing I knew we were leaning over a whole worldful of books and gym stuff and trombone case and our eyes were closing . . .

And then, only then, six days after it started (and it could have lasted six years, I think), did the first kiss come to an end.

Women

It was maybe the first really cold night of the year. I had my gloves on, and a heavy jacket. I was biking home from Marceline's after a marathon game of Scrabble, when I spotted somebody in the shadows with a pair of shoulders like a gorilla's. Then, as I got closer and he moved under a streetlight, I saw who it was: Rich. I pulled over, but he kept on walking, like he didn't know I was there. He was walking pretty fast, his face straight ahead. I coasted alongside him, even a little in front. A number 36 showed under his open jacket; he had his football shirt on. And shoulder pads. And a football under his arm. Still his head never turned. This dude's got rotten peripheral vision, I thought. I was close enough to hear his pad layers scraping against each other. His breath was choo-chooing out in front of him.

"You got a night practice or something?" I said.

He didn't really turn; he just slid his eyes sideways for a second. "Yeah," he grunted and kept on walking.

"So where's your helmet?"

"Forgot it."

"Pants?"

"It was just a run-through. No contact."

"So why the pads?"

No answer. He kept on walking. We were a block from his house. I pulled my bike onto the sidewalk and blocked his way. He stopped. That's when I saw the No-Glare, the black goop that football players smear under each eye to help keep out the glare of the sun. He didn't try to go around. He knew there was no way he was getting home without forking over a couple answers. We stared at each other, no blinks. Little by little his face changed, from a nothing-look to a something-look, the old Richie-look.

"I was at Cricket's," he said.

"Cricket's!"

He bounced the football off my front tire. "That's what I said."

"Football practice, huh?"

"I lied."

"So what were you doing at Cricket's?"

His grin turned to a smirk, and the smirk said, We weren't playing Scrabble, pal. In fact, every-thing about him — the way he was standing, all cocky, tossing the ball in the air, flexing his shoulders, the No-Glare — was one big announcement: You can forget your little bedroom scene with Marcy — me and Cricket are back in first place.

"Okay," I said, "let me put it this way. What were you doing at Cricket's with *that* stuff on?"

"She likes it."

"She *likes* it?"

"Football suits turn her on."

"You can't turn her on in regular clothes?"

He looked at the football like it was Cricket's face. I thought he was going to kiss it. "I can turn her on any time I want. This just does it a little better. She goes a little apeshit."

"Yeah?"

He *did* kiss the ball. "Yeah."

I tried to picture Cricket going apeshit. First I saw her bulldogging Richie onto the living-room rug, then under the rug — humpy, undulating rug; groans. Then I saw her whipping all her clothes off and jumping on top of the TV and throwing her arms out and her head back and yelling: "Yaaaaaaaahhh!" When I tried to picture Marceline going apeshit, the screen went blank.

"Okay," I said, "but *No-Glare?*"

He shrugged. He kept flipping the ball to himself. He looked like he was ready to say something, but he didn't. Then he did. "She likes guys . . . y'know?"

"No. I figured she likes polar bears."

He just looked at me for a while, his mouth a sad-type smile. With his shoulders all puffed up to his ears, he looked inflated, like any second he was going to start floating up to the streetlamp. He wagged his head and gave a short chuckle. "You wouldn't understand." He started off for his house.

Watching him from behind, I could almost feel

those pumped-up shoulders trying to tug his feet off the ground. He wasn't walking, he was drifting. I started laughing. Loud.

He stopped, turned. "What's so funny?"

"I understand," I gasped, "what a joke you look like."

He came drifting back to the bike, blinking, half-smiling. I beat down the temptation to check if his feet were still on the ground.

"Herkimer —" he let out a long, misty breath, "some women —"

"*Women?*" I howled.

The blinking speeded up, but the half-smile never changed. He waited till I stopped laughing. "Some girls . . . like . . . real guys. They like guys that ain't afraid to get dirty." He spun the ball in the air a couple times, started grinning privately to himself. "Know when she started liking me, man?"

"Can't imagine."

"Remember the Marple game?"

"In the mud?"

"Yeah, that one. Well, when I came off the field after the game, I was covered with mud. Every inch of me. Solid mud. Remember?"

"No."

"Well, I was. A mud man. And she told me later, that's when it happened."

"What happened?"

"She started liking me. She said I looked like an animal."

He stopped talking and blinked at me, like I was supposed to say something. Like, Gee, an animal, that's terrific! I tried to imagine Marceline swooning because I looked like an animal. I said, "I think what we're talking here is a little perversion, that's what I think."

This time he did the howling. He staggered around for half a minute. "Man," he said, "what we're talking here is hormones. What we're talking is what happens when a chick with some heavy 'mones gets together with a dude with some equally heavy 'mones." The way he looked at me, I knew he wanted me to ask him *what* happens, but I wouldn't give him the satisfaction. So he spiraled the ball up toward the streetlamp and yelled: "Ooouuu-*wee!*"

"Wow," I went, "wish I had hormones."

His face got all serious. He gave the ball a last look and tucked it under his arm. "Hey look, man, I ain't saying that. All I'm saying is . . ." His eyes rolled to the sky. "Okay . . . Heather Newsome, okay?"

"Yeah."

"Okay. Me and Heather, we were making out this once. Over at 7-Eleven."

"Back of the Dumpster."

He stared. "How'd you know?"

"I was hiding in the Dumpster." He boggled. "Just joking. That's where I made out with her once too."

He slapped the ball. "Okay. Great. So you know

what I'm talking about. I mean, it was no big deal, right?"

I didn't say anything. I wasn't sure what answer would do me the most good.

"Anyway," he said, "it was no big deal for me. Wham, bam, thank you, ma'am. And that's what I'm thinking the next couple days, like, hey, this making out stuff, it's no big thing, y'know? I mean, it was okay and all, but it wasn't better than football." He flipped the ball to me. I flipped it back. "And then . . . and *then* . . . Cricket and me. The Bushes. And all of a sudden, man, it *was* a big deal. Back with Heather, I was thinking, Well, man, I guess you're just not ready yet. I guess all your 'mones didn't kick in yet. But, see what I'm saying, they *were* there the whole time. It just took a Cricket to crank 'em up. And the thing is, man, once your 'mones get cranked up, there's no cranking 'em down. They take over. They take you on a ride you wouldn't be-*lieve*, baby. You don't care if you *never* see another football."

He stopped talking and just looked at me. His eyebrows went up, his lips puckered, he whistled, inhaling-style. He kept it up. I knew what he was doing. He was sending me a message. His eyebrows and his whistle were telling me what he and Cricket did. But I couldn't decode the language. And I didn't want to. What did I care about him and his damn hormones? I was glad now that I had never told him that nothing had happened in Marceline's bedroom.

I was starting to see something about this sex stuff. It's kind of like football. You can't just score a touchdown and then relax and stop trying, because the other team will catch up and pass you. You have to keep scoring and scoring to stay ahead. The stuff that you do with the girl is only the first part; the other part is what you say to the guys afterward. In fact, I was starting to think maybe that was the most important part. I felt like taking that football and ramming it down that puckered whistle of his.

And then I was laughing again, laughing like hell. The pucker flattened out, the eyebrows came down.

"What's so funny now?"

I shook my head. "You, man!"

He pulled away. He took a deep breath, sending his shoulder pads practically over his head. I howled.

"Jerk," he said. He kicked my front tire and floated off.

I stayed there laughing under the streetlight until he disappeared up his driveway. And even then I couldn't stop. I bounced down off the curb, wobbled, and pedaled for home. Chuckle-balls kept bursting out. It was even colder now, freezing, ice at my throat. One second I was laughing, the next I was shaking so bad I could hardly steer. My teeth sounded like Jewel's castanets. In my mind I reached for the second kiss. It wasn't there.

French

Kiss No. 3 came the next day. It took about two days to wear off. Pretty good, but not as long as No. 1 or No. 2.

Kiss No. 4 was special in a different way. It happened on the corner of Princeton and Darby, on the way to school. I just stopped her and did it.

She was so surprised she didn't close her eyes. But she didn't try to stop me. "Hey," she said, "it's morning."

"No kidding."

"I can still taste Honey Smacks in my mouth."

"That's not Honey Smacks," I winked. "That's me."

"Makes me feel married." She scowled. "Mornings are for wives."

"Good morning, Mrs. Herkimer."

"Not just yet, buster." She started walking. But she was grinning.

After school, another kiss. Two in one day. Another first.

That night something else happened that was new. As usual, when I turned the light out and went to bed, I thought about Marceline. About us. But this time, instead of thinking about the *last* kiss, I thought about the *next* one. I thought about it pretty good. I mean, it was *happening*. She was *there*.

Maybe that's why, when we kissed the next day, it seemed a little like a rerun. I mean, it was good. Great, in fact. But not brand, spanking, totally new. And not long-lasting, like the first couple. By now, each kiss was pretty much over when our lips came apart.

So, the only way to keep a kiss going was to keep our lips plastered together. Which we did. When we could. I was getting pretty good at keeping it going, breathing through my nose. I prayed I wouldn't get a cold. One kiss lasted for around five minutes. It happened during a break in a Scrabble game. But the really big thing was, it was the first one in her house.

But you can only keep a kiss going for so long. So, if life couldn't be one big never-ending kiss, the next-best thing was for it to be lots of littler kisses. Which is what happened. Some days. The best day of all being the Friday after Thanksgiving. We were with each other from ten in the morning till nine at night, most of it at the mall. I bet we did a hundred kisses that day. We'd look in a shoe shop, kiss, look in a girls' store, kiss, buy a donut, kiss, take a bite, kiss . . .

But most days we couldn't be together that much. And when we did see a lot of each other, we were usually in school. Now, for a lot of people, that's no problem. It's not unusual to see a couple trading spit in the middle of a hallway. But Marceline, she couldn't handle school hallways. So, if anything was going to happen at school, it was going to happen in a deserted cranny somewhere. We went looking a couple times, but by the time we found a cranny she approved of, the bell was ringing for next class.

What all I'm saying is, we carried your basic liplock about as far as it could go. I knew it was time to move on the day we were halfway through a kiss and I suddenly realized we both had our mouths open. Not much. Not gapers, like you see some kids in the hallways, two pythons trying to swallow each other whole. But still: open. Damn, I'm thinking, what do we have here? Should I or shouldn't I?

There was a lot to think about. Starting with, did Marceline realize her mouth was open? I mean, maybe she was like me, just getting into it and relaxing and having a good time, and her jaw just sort of slacked open without her even knowing it. One thing I did know — I wouldn't try to take her by surprise, not if I wanted to come back out with a complete tongue.

But, man, it was tempting. Just knowing it was there . . . open. And anyway, what if — what *if* — she *did* know? What if it was an invitation?

Well, I had to find out, I had to know for sure. I started dragging my tongue up from its cranny. It didn't want to come. No way did it want to meet up with another tongue. Well, I could be stubborn too. Pretty soon I had it straightening out, crawling past the molars, past the fang teeth, up to my front teeth, even a little past my front teeth, right out to my lip line . . . nothing, nobody there. Just then the kiss ended, Marceline pulled away, and there I was, with my mouth open and the tip of my tongue peeking out. It shot back like a turtle into its shell. I prayed Marceline hadn't noticed.

The next time, her lips were clamped down pretty tight. That's when I started into some pretty serious thinking ahead.

It was kind of scary at first, even though it was only happening in my head. I was nervous, just like that first time at the movies. Finally, on my sixth or seventh imagined try at a French kiss, I was almost there — and she disappeared — leaving my tongue flapping in my fantasy like a lizard's. It kept happening: I'd be almost there, and *poof*, she was gone. Like my brain wasn't strong enough to hold the molecules of her image together.

But I kept trying, and finally it happened. After that, it was easy. One night I even dreamed we were French-kissing, really getting into it. Just as I was going to try something else . . . reaching . . . reaching . . . I woke up. My body felt fizzy, like a soda down-foaming after being poured too fast. Probably my hormones settling back down, I figured.

The dream was so real. When I saw Marceline at

school that day, I couldn't help thinking she knew, like her dream-self had gone back to her and reported what had happened. I almost flinched, in case she was going to slap me. But she didn't. She was her same old self. And maybe even more. The more time I spent with her that day, the closer I seemed to get to her dream-self. Maybe that's why, when I tried to French-kiss her after school, I was so surprised at what happened.

In my imagining, the French kiss always went great. But out by the bike rack that day, she pulled away when I tried it.

"What's the matter?" I said.

She shrugged and rolled her eyes to the sky and made a fishy, goofy kind of face that gave me an idea of what she must have looked like in third grade. But she didn't say anything, just went on shrugging and grinning.

So I pulled her back and tried again. Her lips were clamped tight. I tunneled through them and — *bam!* — the Berlin Wall. Her teeth. But I didn't give up. I pushed, pushed. I wondered if there were some kind of tongue exercises I should have been doing to get ready for this. I could feel our whole bodies tensing, clenching, all our muscles funneled to the spot where the tip of my tongue was colliding with her front teeth. I think one of us grunted; I'm not sure who. I opened my eyes — smack into hers. There we were: all tongue and teeth and eyeballs.

The rack shook — somebody was getting his bike out. She pulled away and went back to the goofy grin. Over her shoulder, in the distance, up against a big tree with spotted bark, Richie and Cricket were magnetizing themselves to each other.

I let go of her. "Cripes, you'd think I was trying to rape ya."

The goofy grin disappeared. "I think I know what a rape is."

We glared at each other. I couldn't think of anything to say. I felt really crummy. Embarrassed. Having to fight just to get a French kiss from my own girlfriend — and losing. Plus, my tongue ached.

And there were Richie and Cricket under the spotted tree, rubbing my face in it. Marceline looked over at them, then back at me. "I'm not Cricket."

"Who said you were?"

"Jason — I just — I don't like to be pushed. Except for my mother and father, nobody's ever made me do things I didn't want to do."

"So that's it, you don't want to."

"Well . . ."

The goofy grin was back.

"You *do* want to."

I moved forward. She stepped back. "I'm not exactly saying *that*."

We stared some more. And then, half surprising me, my feet turned and started carrying me away.

"Aren't we walking home together?"

Her voice behind me sounded surprised, amazed.

Like, What does what just happened have to do with us going home together? Like, I can't believe you're really walking away from me.

Well, believe it, baby. "Forget it," I called, and I kept on walking. And I didn't look back, not once the whole way home, even though my eyes were burning and I was shaking like a leaf.

The phone rang just after dinner.

"Jason?"

"Yeah."

"I'm sorry." I didn't say anything. "Jason? You there?"

"Yeah."

"I'm sorry."

"I heard."

"Believe me?"

"Why should I?" Silence. Careful, dude. She'll apologize, but she'll never crawl. "I guess."

"Jason?"

"Huh?"

"Want to come over tonight?"

"A school night?"

"My mother said okay. I can finish my algebra in fifteen minutes, and I can do my English in study hall tomorrow morning. What do you say?"

"I don't know if I'm allowed."

"The Scrabble board is out."

"I'll ask."

I asked. My mother's eyebrows went up. Ham

just kept reading the script of the new play he's going to be in. His head twitched and his lips moved silently.

"Scrabble?" my mother said, like she'd never heard the word. She was clipping coupons from a magazine.

"Yeah. We play all the time. You know it."

"It's a school night."

I hate it when parents try to duck a question by throwing some obvious, unconnected detail back in your face. Like I was supposed to go, "Oh golly, that's right. I forgot. How stupid of me. I withdraw the question."

I stared at her. "So?"

"Jason, you know we have a rule."

"Man," I said, "a couple weeks ago you sounded like I wasn't seeing her enough. Now you're saying we can't play a dumb game of Scrabble."

She stopped clipping. "It's not Scrabble I'm talking about." She gave me her what's-the-truth-behind-your-words look.

I felt like grabbing a lamp and smashing it against a wall. Why can't they just believe you? But I stayed cool. "So what's the problem?"

She stared some more. I knew by her face that she was weakening. She wanted help from Ham. She started clipping coupons again. She was hoping I had taken my best shot and would go now.

"She's on the phone, waiting," I said.

The scissors stopped. "Are her parents home?"

"No. They went to Florida. They left the whole house to her. The refrigerator's fulla beer."

Mistake, I groaned to myself. I'd given her a way out, and she snapped it up. "Okay, smart alec, you can stay home then."

Ham's voice came across the room. "Let him go." His face was still in the script. Was he speaking one of his lines?

"Why?" said my mother.

"Slack."

"How about setting a precedent? Next week it'll be two nights."

"He's doing it for us."

"Really? That's interesting."

"He desires to exercise his mind and improve his vocabulary. Hence, the pursuit of Scrabble. He knows that a couple more years of intense mind-enhancement could qualify him for academic scholarships to college, and that would ease our financial burden in securing for him a higher education. So you see —" for the first time he looked up from his script — "he's doing it for us."

My mother didn't exactly look grateful. "You're saying he can go?"

Ham nodded and went back to his script.

Three seconds later I was at the phone. "Okay," I said.

"What took you so long?"

"Nothin'. It's okay."

"Okay. Great. Seeya."

"Seeya."
I hung up. I felt like Christmas.

Fifteen minutes later, across the Scrabble board on her kitchen table, with the sound of her mother's footsteps heading upstairs and her father out of the house shopping for snow tires, I was doing what she wouldn't let me do that afternoon.

Neck

We were in the movies. At the mall. Saturday matinee. I was feeling great. Relaxed. Thinking about how good things had gotten since *The Dead Never Sleep*. This time it was Jason and Marceline who didn't wait until the main feature. (Although Marceline did insist on waiting till the lights went out. And we used two seats.) I don't even remember what the feature was. Like I said, things were great. We were cruising. Until.

I felt her finger in my chest, pushing. "Hey," she whispered, "what are you doing?"

"What do you mean?"

"I mean, *what* are you *doing?*"

"What do you think I was doing?"

"You tell me."

She knew damn well what I was doing. "I was kissing you," I said.

"Is that all?"

"What's that s'posed to mean?"

"If I went to the ladies' room right now and looked in the mirror, would I just happen to find a purple blotch on my neck?"

I swept my arm toward the aisle. "Be my guest. Go look."

She stared at me for a minute, her eyes gleaming in the movie glow. "Jason, no hickeys."

I guess I should have dropped the whole thing there, but I didn't. "What's wrong with hickeys?"

"I just don't want any." Now I did the staring and glaring. She repeated: "No. Hickeys."

"Why not?"

"I just *told* you. I don't *want* any."

"*Why* don't you want any?"

"What business is it of yours?"

She glared. I glared. My glare said: We were just French-kissing a minute ago. Doesn't that make it my business?

She read it. She blinked. "I just don't happen to want purple blotches all over me. That's all."

"Who's talking all over you? We're talking one. That's all."

"I don't want *any*. Not one."

I gave her my you-gotta-be-crazy look. She turned her face to the screen, sniffed.

She knew I was staring at her, but she never flinched. One of the many hard-to-figure things about Marceline, she doesn't mind being stared at. She was so still, so straight, so . . . *Marceline*, it seemed the movie was watching her. And more than ever I wanted to give her one. Somewhere inside me an achiness was growing, like a little somebody waking up and stretching away stiffness. Here we were, not even touching, and I was feeling more than ever before. No . . . not really feeling more . . . feeling different. The other feelings I had had about Marceline were sort of eye feelings and brain feelings and skin feelings. I could think about them. If I had to, I could have written something about them for English class. But this feeling, this achiness, it was down lower, deeper, somewhere around the stomach, and there were no words for it. In fact, I'm not even sure it was a feeling. It was just something . . . *happening* . . . way inside me, something aching, stretching, wishing, like against the inner walls of a rubbery bubble, trying to get out, trying to hatch, trying, trying . . . The arms of my seat were wet under my hands.

I said, "Marceline, are you my girlfriend?"

Shadows of screen glow shifted across her face. After a long time she answered. "I guess you could say that."

"Okay," I said, "so, you're somebody's girlfriend. You're *supposed* to have a hickey. Everybody does. What's the big deal?"

The movie glow peeled from her face as she turned slowly to me. "I'm. Not. Every. Body."

We just sat there then, staring at each other for about a week. A lot of ideas went through my head, but what finally came out of my mouth was something I didn't think about at all: "Well then, how about *you* giving *me* one?"

She laughed so loud she shocked herself. Her hand

shot to her mouth, and she started shaking with muffled squeals. I got up and left.

I walked around the lobby for a while. Then I sat down on a red padded bench under a mirror. Let her come to me. Why the hell am I putting up with all this anyway? That day at the bike rack, now this. Who needs it? Who ever heard of a girl like this?

I shivered, thinking how Richie would howl if he heard about what had just happened. Some days Cricket came to school with her neck so blue, from a distance it looked like she was wearing a turtleneck. Was she complaining? Was she too high and mighty? I couldn't stand the thought of ever facing Marceline again. I cursed myself for not being sixteen yet. Then I'd have my own wheels, and I'd take off, baby, trot right on outta this joint and out to the parking lot, where my Trans Am would be waiting — black, babes, with mag wheels — and I'd be gone.

A couple came giggling through the swinging doors, up out of the darkness. The movie was ending. I panicked. I jumped up and went back in. She was still there. Smiling. But not laughing anymore. We didn't pull apart till after the lights went on.

Ovulation

Mimi Hykendahl is one of the friendliest girls around. The cheery type. Always laughing, smiling, making jokes.

In Algebra, Mimi sits in front of Richie. They're always doing stuff to each other. It usually starts with Richie trying to stick something down her back or snapping her bra strap, stuff like that. Once he slipped a whoopee cushion onto her seat just before she sat down. Nobody in the class laughed louder or longer than Mimi herself.

One day Richie came to school with a pocketful of little round white things, like dried peas or something. He said they were tapioca pearls. So naturally, in Algebra, about five minutes into the class, he tosses one into Mimi's hair. It stays. She never feels it. Next one bounces off her hair and rolls across the floor. She looks down. She knows something's going on. When the next one lands in her hair, instead of turning and starting some kind of funny feud with Rich, like she usually does, she just slashes

her hand through her hair till the tapiocas come out.
So naturally Richie bombards her with more. Again
she sweeps them from her hair, and this time she
snaps her hand behind her, like, "Stop bothering
me."

Richie just laughs. So do Calvin and I. We can't
believe she's serious, not Mimi Hykendahl. But when
Richie opens with another tapioca attack, Mimi freezes
the teacher and the whole class by whirling around
and yelling at him: "Knock it off!"

For ten minutes none of us moves a muscle. Then
Richie kicks my foot and whispers, "Rag on."

I look over at Calvin. He nods. His mouth forms
an egg shape, and he whispers real precisely: "Oh-
vyoo-lay-shun."

That's it! I think. That's what Marceline's problem is.

Periods are weird, like a voodoo curse. What they
do is, they make girls a little loony for a while each
month. (I used to think a period lasted five minutes;
now I know it's five days. Except for my sister
Cootyhead. I think she's had hers ever since she
was born.) Like, Dr. Jekyll and Mr. Hyde. Bride
of Frankenstein. They get all emotional. Weepy.
Touchy. You tell them there's a piece of lint on their
sweater, and they start screaming. But mostly, they
get bitchy. Crabby. They don't agree with anything.
Or anybody. And the thing is, it's not really their
fault. They can't help it. Any more than a guy can

help kicking a can that shows up in front of him on the sidewalk.

This was the Monday after the Saturday at the mall movie. If Saturday was the first of her five days, it should be ending by Wednesday.

Thursday I tried again. Out by the big spotted tree.

She pulled away. "*Jay*-son."

"*Now* what's the problem?"

"You tell me. I don't have a problem."

In my head I did a fast recount. Yep, five had passed, all right. "I don't have a problem," I said.

"I thought this was all settled back on Saturday."

"That was Saturday." I pulled her closer. "This is Thursday. Five days later."

She pushed away. We stared at each other, and somewhere in there I knew: it never was her period. It was her.

"Damn," I said, "what do you think I am, Jack the Ripper or something?" I stepped back, spread my arms. "Look, it's me. Jason. Remember me? What are you afraid of?"

She leaned her head back against the tree. "I know who you are, and fear has nothing to do with it."

"Then what —" I kicked the tree; she looked down, with her eyeballs, anyway; her eyebrows stayed up — "*does* have something to do with it?"

She closed her eyes, took a deep breath; inhale, exhale. "I told you."

"Told me what? Huh?" She took another breath. "*Huh?*"

"I don't like them."

"Well, great," I said to her closed eyelids. "Great reason. Makes a lotta sense. Everybody else in the world likes them. *I* like them. I wouldn't mind having one on myself. But who do I get? I gotta get somebody — the *one* person in the universe — who decides she's not gonna like them."

"Call you Hard Luck Harry."

"Yeah, that's it, just make a big joke out of it. Think about yourself. That's all you do, you know. Did it ever occur to you that maybe *your* feelings ain't the only ones that count in this world?"

"Aren't, not ain't."

"Did you ever think about doing something because of somebody else? Just because it would make somebody else feel better, even if you weren't all that crazy about it your personal self? Did it ever occur to you *not* to be selfish? Open your eyes!"

Her eyelids moseyed up like two little shades. But she didn't say anything. Neither did I. I found out it was easier to holler at her with her eyes shut. There was only one thing left to do, one thing that could make me feel better. Go.

I had only gone a couple steps when I heard her sigh and groan. "Oh no —" I stopped, turned. Her eyes were rolled up to the treetops. "He's leaving me again. Every time he gets mad at me, he leaves me."

Oh yeah?

I went back to her. I stood right next to her until she decided to go. I walked her home, right to her front door. I even opened the door for her and bowed as she went in. I'm not saying we talked. Or even looked at each other.

Complications

Why is everything getting so complicated? Why are we always arguing? Why do we spend half the time not speaking to each other? What's happening to Us?

I wish we could go back to October. Back to *The Dead Never Sleep*. Back to the same two seats, the same moment ("Hey —"). Go back and just stay there, staple ourselves to that moment. I wish.

One minute I want to take off in a black Trans Am. The next minute I want to marry her.

Almost every fight we have ends with me walking away. Then, that night or the next day, she calls, and we make up.

I think ahead a lot. About Marceline and me. Doing stuff. I felt kind of guilty at first, and nervous. But now it's pretty easy. Each time I think about us doing one thing, it gets easier to think about the next thing.

Other people are thinking too. Thinking we're doing things. Maybe not It, but things. A hell of a lot more than what we're really doing.

So sometimes it's weird, really strange, when we're

together, by ourselves, not fighting. I have to catch myself, remind myself not to make a grab for her, this is the real Marceline. Because in my head, in other people's heads, we already started, weeks ago. I feel like saying to her, "Look, it's no big deal. Everybody already thinks we're messing around. So what's the difference? We might as well."

But I don't say it, and I don't mess. What's worse, I think we're even starting to go backwards. Sometimes, if my lips aren't planted square on hers, I can feel her getting a little edgy. She's paranoid about me giving her a hickey.

It's ridiculous. In a way, I don't even care anymore. I mean, about the hickey itself. But what I do care about is that she won't let me.

I say this hickey business is the cause of all our problems. She says no. I say let me give her just one little light one, even on the inside of her arm, where nobody can see, and it'll fade away in a day or two, and all our problems will fade along with it, and I'll never ask to give her one again. She says no. So what happens? Sometimes I'll just *pretend* I'm going for her neck. Just to get a reaction out of her. Just to make sure the paranoia is alive and well. Just to start a fight.

And yet — is this wacko, or what? — I can't even go one day without kissing her. I mean, it's not just that I want to. I *have* to. Like, nothing in the day counts until it happens. Then I'm okay. But it's not a real yippee kind of okay, like in the early days. It's more like the big gulp of air you come up for after diving off the deep end and swimming half the pool underwater. You want it, and it feels good, but even more, you can't stand doing without it.

We still play Scrabble, but it's not the same. The scorekeeping gets a little sloppy. If one of us loses by fifty points or more, nobody demands Total Disgrace.

There's going to be a ninth-grade prom. First time in twenty-one years. They made the announcement last week. Everybody is talking about it — except Marceline and me. I know I'm thinking about it, and I'm sure she is too. I guess we're both waiting for the other one to say something first.

Sometimes I wonder what's keeping us together. Every time I take a hike after a fight, I swear we're going to break up. But we don't. Another crazy thing: sometimes it seems that the more we fight and the more miserable we are, the closer we get, and the harder it would be for anything to tear us apart. Sometimes I think it's not us. It's out of our hands. It's outside forces. Destiny. We're meant to be together. Take the prom. I know we'll go together. I know. So I don't mention it. Why mess with destiny?

A lot of this craziness — and something extra — was packed into one night during Christmas vacation. The Y was having a dance for junior-highers. I probably would have gone with Marceline, but she had to go over to Great Valley to try out for the district band, so she'd be late. But she said she'd meet me there. So I went with the guys.

It wasn't too bad. They had an old-fashioned jukebox — one with rainbow lights on the front — and that's what they played the records on. Santa Claus came. I guess nobody ever told him to stay clear of ninth-graders. By the time he escaped, half his beard was off, and what was left had wet candy canes sticking to it; his red-and-white hat was racing around the gym on somebody's head; and two white plastic forks were sticking out of the padding in his butt.

I did one dance, if you want to call it that. The Bunny Hop. When the record first started, you could hardly hear it because of the booing. Then some of the girls got in a snaky line and started doing it. So the guys jumped in too. I was heading for the spot behind Jewel Fiorito, but Peter whipped in in front of me and clamped his hands to her waist. So I got behind Heather Newsome. By the time we got done with the Bunny Hop, it was more like the Elephant Stomp.

But mostly I just hung around, drinking up sodas and sweating it out. It wasn't just that I was anxious to be with her. I had something to give her. A Christmas present. A gold ankle chain. Just like the one Richie gave to Cricket. Like a lot of the girls are wearing. Cost me a lot of lunch money.

By the time she got there, around nine o'clock, I was a nervous wreck.

"Where were you?"

She took off her coat and stuffed her mittens up one sleeve. "I told you." She hugged herself and shivered. "Brrrrr. Cold out. Where can I hang this?"

"Over there. You said you'd be here by eight."

She hung up her coat. She wasn't acting guilty at all. "My parents wanted to go out for dinner, so we went out for dinner."

"*This* late?"

"Then we drove around looking at the Christmas displays. Did you ever see the one in Drexel Hill, a couple blocks from the hospital? Oh, you wouldn't believe it. Cars all over the place. We had to park two blocks away and walk back to look."

"Great," I said. "I'm glad you had a good time, while I was here waiting for you."

For the first time she looked straight at me. "Jason, I was with my parents. What did you want me to do?"

"You could have told them you had a dance to go to."

"Why? They brought me here. Look." She spun around, like a model, big smile. "Here I am."

I hate it when she tries to laugh things off. I glared — "Yeah, late" — and wiped the big smile away.

"Jason, my parents are good to me. I do love them. I like to be with *them* sometimes too. Are you saying you don't want to share me with my parents?"

I felt like saying a lot of things, but I couldn't. I couldn't even think straight. Why did it bother me when she said, "I do love them?" What should I do? I couldn't walk away. Not here. Not when she just came. And I couldn't answer her question. Not honestly, anyway. So I did the only thing left to do. I grabbed her hand and pulled her out to the dance floor.

It was a slow dance. Right away everything was different. Than ever before. We were close. Up till then it was usually just our mouths that got close; from there on down, we sort of angled away from each other. There always seemed to be something between us: books, trombone case, Scrabble board, chair arm, winter coats. Now, for the first time, we were both vertical, facing each other, with nothing between us but a couple millimeters of cloth. It was like all of a sudden our mouths stretched to the floor — our whole bodies were kissing. Every other time I took a step, I felt the front of her leg with the front of my leg. It made me kind of dizzy and a little scared at the same time.

Then the something extra happened. I felt her leg, but this time it wasn't my leg that did the feeling. It was something else. Something between. Something that had been before, but hadn't been so much before. Hadn't been *there. Out.* Like a lower nose. Like it had felt left out, and wanted to be close, too.

I stayed close on top, but from the waist on down I pulled back like a bulldog was snapping at me. Did she feel it? Did she know it wasn't my leg? Can the girl tell? What is she thinking? Can she feel my heart? Why am I getting out of breath? What happens next?

The music stopped. We came apart, almost with a smacking *pop*, I was so clammy. I walked behind her as we left the dance area. I steered her toward the shadows. I found a chair, sat down, leaned forward with my elbows on my knees, shielded myself till I came back to normal. I kept remembering Richie on hormones: "They take you on a ride you wouldn't be-*lieve*."

We danced a couple more times — fast ones . . . and left early. She wondered why we were walking the long way, past the school. "Just to be out longer together," I told her. But when I started to steer her toward The Bushes, she got that oh-no look on her face. I thought we were in for another fight. We stood there staring at each other. We went over the same old arguments, only this time with our eyes instead of our voices. Finally she shrugged and sighed and marched straight into The Bushes. Not a word had been said.

She was waiting with her arms folded. She wasn't exactly overjoyed. You can lead a girl to bushes, but you can't make her make out. Well, that was okay, because that wasn't the only thing I had planned anyway. I took the little gold-wrapped box out of my pocket. I smiled. "Merry Christmas."

In the bushy shadows, her eyes were the only part of her face that I could clearly see. They stared at the box, then at me. I grabbed one of her arms, pulled off the mitten, and put the box in her hand. "It's not gonna explode."

"It's not Christmas yet," she said.

"Open it," I said.

She pulled her other mitten off and started opening it. It took her about a half hour, untying the bow, unpeeling the Scotch tape. (I had pictured her tearing into it.) When it was finally open, she just stared at it some more.

"It's an ankle chain," I said.

"Like Cricket's," she said. Her voice was raspy, whispery.

"Yeah," I said. "Real gold. Fourteen karat."

Just then there was a cough. A girl-cough. It wasn't Marceline. I turned. Somebody else was in The Bushes. At the other end. About ten feet away. I couldn't see them.

When I turned back, I knew something was wrong. Even though I couldn't see her face, and even though she didn't move or make a sound, I knew she was crying. We just stood and stood, our icy breaths puffing into each other. The only part of me moving were my frozen toes in my shoes. I think I thought if we stood there long enough, the whole crummy night would start to turn itself around. She would pick up the chain and swing it in the moonlight and go, "Ooooo, Jason, it's bee-yoooo-tiful!" and throw her arms around my neck.

But it didn't happen. And it wasn't going to. All there was was a short girl-cough every once in a while and a faint rustle of bushes. She wasn't going to make anything easy for me. She wasn't even going to be the one to say, "We'd better go now," like she usually did. So, finally, I said it.

I was about halfway across the lawn before she caught up to me. Her hands were in her pockets. When we got to the sidewalk I looked back. The others were coming out of The Bushes. They were heading in another direction, but as they moved into the full moonlight I could tell who they were: Peter and Jewel.

I was numb from the cold — and from more than the cold.

Merry Christmas.

Fight

"Fight!"

No need to ask where — you just stampede along with the herd. For fire drills they should yell "Fight!" over the intercom. Set a record for clearing out a building.

It was after school. First week back from Christmas vacation. In the parking lot. The mob was cheering like somebody was on a never-ending touchdown run. Guys and girls were standing on the hoods and roofs of teachers' cars. One guy on a roof had a girl propped on his shoulders. Her eyes were bulging, and the thumb of one red-mittened hand was clamped between her teeth.

When I finally drilled my way through the mob, my first thought was, Damn, another one of those. Because the two fighters weren't really fighting at all. They were on the ground, and they weren't moving an inch. They were just in the old death clinch that some dummies call a fight. It was weird. All the action — guys jabbing and weaving, girls hopping up and down on car tops, the howling — was in the audience.

The two so-called fighters were so wrapped up in each other that I couldn't even tell who they were. Plus, one of them had a leather jacket on that was draped over both their heads. The only thing that impressed me was that one of them had taken his jacket off, because it was thirty degrees out.

The mob ring got so tight that the people on the inside were practically looking straight down. I was ready to go meet Marceline for our usual walk home, when the clinch sprang out a leg here, an arm there, like a motor grinding to life, and suddenly it was churning and grunting and body-whipping across the asphalt. The mob circle opened like water hit by a stone. The two heads came out from under the jacket. I almost croaked: it was Peter Kim and Mike Vesto. Then I saw their mouths. Both sets of teeth were red. It was a real fight after all.

The mob exploded into an even bigger frenzy. All over, guys were bobbing and weaving and jabbing, calling out stuff, like "Uppercut! Uppercut!" and then throwing uppercuts to demonstrate. One puny little seventh-grader went apeshit, jumping around and flinging his arms and legs until he finally smacked a girl behind him right in the teeth. The girl lurched backward — the mob gave a little, like a pillow — and ran off bawling. A ninth-grader knuckled the back of the seventh-grader's gourd, and the kid never

moved after that. But other seventh-graders —
Rudolph-belt was one of them — were laughing hys-
terically at the fight.

"Good fight, huh?"

Richie was standing beside me.

"Yeah," I said.

But I didn't believe it. Now that one of my best
friends was involved, the word "good" didn't seem
to belong with the word "fight." Even though it had
all the things that had always made a fight good —
two fighters not afraid to tear into each other; lots
of roundhouse swinging, like colliding helicopters;
every once in a while a fist actually landing on a face
(with a smacked-meat sound nothing at all like you
hear in the movies or TV); and, most of all, blood —
it wasn't good. Maybe it was even a great fight; but
it definitely wasn't good.

Then it was over. Whistles split the air, the mob
cracked open, and the wrestling and basketball
coaches charged into the battle and grabbed the
fighters. Groans and boos thundered over the parking lot. Peter and Vesto were led away. Somebody
handed Peter his jacket. Vesto was wiping the blood
from his face. Peter didn't bother. It seemed like
they ought to be screaming at each other, but
they didn't say a word, didn't even look at each
other.

Richie and I moved out with the mob. Everybody
was buttoning up their jackets.

"What was it about?" I said.

Richie smirked. "Fiorito."

"Jewel?"

"Yeah."

"Like what?"

"Like Vesto said something about her, and Peter didn't like it."

"Wha'd he say?"

Richie shrugged, smirked. "I don't know. Take a guess."

It wasn't hard to guess. No matter how many ways you talked about Jewel, the message always came out the same: big boobs and hot to trot.

Richie bobbed and weaved in front of me, grazed my chin with a right cross. "Later, man."

In a couple seconds he was wrapped around Cricket down by the buses.

I headed for where I always met Marceline after school. She was gone. I started after her, but it was Peter who was on my mind. He kept surprising me. First, by going out with Jewel. I mean, I had always figured that whatever his type was, it wasn't Jewel. When you thought of Jewel Fiorito, you thought of a girl that got passed from bush to bush. In fact, when you thought of her, you didn't even think of a girl, really. Not a complete, whole girl. Like, down the hallway comes a pair of balloons — one is named Jewel, the other Fiorito. But then I figured, shoot, there's not a guy in school who wouldn't like to get his hands on those babies, so why should I expect Peter to be any different. Go for it, P.K.

But even that didn't get me ready for this last surprise, that Peter would fight over her. And fight Vesto, of all people. When you fight Vesto, you fight his leather jacket, his car, the hair on his chest. And from what I saw, Peter might have even been winning. A nasty question kept jabbing me: Would I fight for Marceline? Damn right. Bloody mouth and all? Sure. Fight Vesto? Believe it.

Marceline was halfway home when I caught up to her. "Hey, you didn't wait."

She sent me a small smile but kept looking ahead. "I waited."

"Yeah, how long?"

"About ten seconds."

"I figured."

"I knew you were at the brawl."

"You saw me?"

"I didn't have to. I knew." She faced me just long enough to say, "I knew you wouldn't want to miss it."

I grinned to myself because of what she didn't know. "Too bad. You missed a great fight."

"I'm crushed."

"Blood all over the place."

"Swell."

"You *do* know who was fighting, don't you?"

" 'Fraid not."

Dramatic pause. "Peter and Vesto."

She stopped. Her head snapped around, eyes wide. "Peter?"

"Yep. Peter Herbert Kim."

She started walking but kept looking at me. At least, she started out looking at me, and then it was more like through me. Her eyes seemed to finally settle a couple blocks behind my head. "Jewel."

It wasn't a question. It was a statement.

"Huh?"

Her eyes came back to me. "It was over Jewel."

"Yeah. How'd you know?"

She shrugged, looked ahead. "Just thought so."

"Vesto said something. About Jewel."

"I can imagine."

I chuckled. "Yeah, me too."

She gave me a stare that speared the chuckle in my throat. "I'll bet, you too."

"Hey —" my voice crawled up past the dead chuckle — "wha'd *I* do?"

She turned away. We walked a block in silence, past the Methodist church where my floppy shoelace had led to our second kiss. At last she said something. "Peter was at my house last night."

You could have knocked me over with a french fry.

Her eyes locked into mine. "Surprised?"

I ripped my eyes away. "Why should I be?"

"You want to hear something funny? Huh?" She nudged me, smiling. At first I thought she was being cutesy-friendly; then I realized it only looked that way. "Jewel doesn't know what all you guys say about her. She doesn't know she has a whole other life that all your lies have made up for her."

"*My* lies?"

"You believe them, don't you? You believe she did it with Michael Vesto, don't you? I mean, after all, Michael Vesto *said* so, right? You believe everything your pal Richie Bell *says* about her, don't you? Maybe somebody should tell her. She thinks all she did was make out with a couple guys. Isn't that funny?" Another nudge, harder. "Huh? Maybe somebody should fill her in, so she won't have to go around not knowing who she really is. Poor thing."

Her lips clamped shut. Frosty breath came in quick puffs from her red nose. When she spoke again, her voice was quieter, slower. "I like Jewel. Jewel is nice. She's a person. A good person. And I didn't need Peter to tell me that. She really likes Peter. Peter likes her. Really likes her." Her mouth looked ready to say more, but nothing came out.

We walked on. Why was I feeling shaky? We were coming to the corner where we split to go to our own houses.

I cleared my throat. "Marceline . . . I was thinking about the prom —"

"Jason."

She was shaking her head. I shut up. She looked at me, then all around, like for something she couldn't find. Her eyes were gleaming. She shivered, crushed her books to her chest, jerked her head away. "See you tomorrow." She crossed the street.

Quark

How did it happen? In fact, *did* it happen? I'm not even sure of that. I keep expecting her to be there after school, waiting to walk home. Each time the phone rings, I can't believe it's not her. I think any minute, any second now, I'll wake up.

She acted kind of funny for a couple weeks. I'd be kissing her, and next thing I knew there'd be tears in her eyes. She couldn't go to the mall (sick) or the movies (homework). Every day I looked down, hoping to see the chain on her ankle. It was never there. I was afraid to ask why.

We still played Scrabble — as long as I called up and asked to come over. The white slab of the fluorescent light glared above our heads. The kitchen that was one of our main kissing places became about as cozy as a dentist's office. And that's where it happened.

I had just laid down QUARK (subatomic particle) over the Triple Word Score space on the bottom center. It was a chance I had waited for for years. The ten-point Q on a Double Letter Score space (twenty points), plus the whole word (twenty-eight) tripled.

"Eighty-four," I said, trying not to sound too braggy. She wrote it down without raising an eyebrow. So I said, "Could be an all-time record for one word. Y'think?"

She kept looking at the scorepad, her pencil tracing the *84* over and over. I figured she was trying to remember if she had ever had a bigger one-word score. But when she finally said something, it wasn't about that at all. Her pencil stopped. Her eyes were still on the pad. "Jason . . . I think . . . maybe . . . we should stop seeing each other."

Silence. My eyelids screeched against my eyeballs. The pure, white slab overhead turned glacier-cold. Her eyes — just her eyes — came up from the scorepad. "Jason?"

I smiled, shrugged. "Okay, so it's *not* an all-time record." I took QUARK off the board. "Prob'ly didn't spell it right anyway."

"Oh jeez —" She swung away from me and up from her chair, her hand at her face. She went to the sink, ran some water, took a drink, tore off a paper towel, blew her nose, threw the paper towel into the basket, took another drink, came back, sat down. Her nose and eyes were red. She got back up, stood by the refrigerator, leaned her head against it. "Jason . . . we can't . . . I . . . it's not working. I'm not —" she walked around the kitchen, aching, straining at something; she stopped in front of me, looked down in pain — "*happy*. I'm never *happy* anymore." The way she said the word, it seemed extinct. She waited, blinking. "Are you?"

"Sure," I said.

"No you're not."

"I am so. How do you know how happy I am?"

"Jason."

"Come to think of it, I'm about the happiest dude I know of. Leastways, I was till I put that damn word down."

If there's such a thing as a soft scream, she let one out.

"*Jay*-son. It's not 'quark.' It's us."

She ripped off another paper towel.

"What's wrong with us?" I asked.

"Hah!" She blew her nose, threw the towel away, ripped off another. "Don't you *tell* me you're happy. Is that why you're always stomping off? Because you're so delighted with me?"

"Not always, I don't."

She looked at her hands, surprised to find a towel in them. She threw it away. She scowled at me, hands on hips, left the kitchen, came back with something shiny — the ankle chain — in her hand. She dropped it onto the board. "Tell me you're happy about all the money you spent for this, and I never wear it."

I shrugged. "That's your business. I was just happy to give it to you."

"Oh really?" She picked up the chain. "So then you wouldn't mind if I just sent it down the garbage disposal." She glared. I didn't answer. Her face sagged. The chain fell back to the board. She sat down. "Jason, it bothers you that I don't wear the chain. It hurts you. I know it does. I'm not saying it shouldn't. It hurts me too."

"So," I said, "what's the problem?"

"The problem is that I am not an ankle-chain girl. Wearing one of those things would make me feel —" she stared at it like it was a snake — "I don't know . . . it's hard to explain . . . like a slave. A prisoner. To me, it would feel like I was dragging around a ball and chain. Jason's prisoner." She stopped, seemed to be waiting for me to say something. I was going to say, "Is that so bad?" but I didn't. She made a dopey grin. "I know, I'm weird. Say it."

I tried. Really.

Her eyes widened. Her lip quivered. "Oh, Jason, please don't look so sad."

I smiled. "Okay."

She slumped, got up, tore off another towel, crumpled it, threw it away, went to the stove. "Jason, we don't have fun anymore. We never laugh anymore. All we do is . . . is . . . make out and fight, fight and make out."

"And play Scrabble."

She smiled. "Yeah, right. That *was* a great word. You can have the record."

"I'd rather," I said, forcing myself to look straight at her, "have you." She went to the sink, took two more paper towels, didn't use them on her face, just crumpled them and threw them away. They were starting to show above the rim of the basket. "If I knew making out with me bothered you that much —"

She turned, shaking her head. "No, Jason, don't say that. I'm not *that* weird. I like making out. Maybe I'm not a nymphomaniac, but I do enjoy it. I'm normal. That way, anyway."

"So, what's the problem?"

She took a deep breath, looked around the ceiling, crumpled a paper towel, shrugged. "Pressure, I guess."

"Huh?"

"I feel pressure. All the time."

"What for? From?"

She hesitated, peeped it, like a question: "You?"

"Me? What do you mean?"

"I mean, I feel pressure from you."

"I don't attack you."

"I know."

"So?"

"You're . . . I . . . always feel you're not satisfied with me. I never used to worry about myself before, about what other people thought. I thought I was pretty okay. But now, I don't know, I feel like a rat all the time. I go around feeling guilty because I'm always making you miserable."

I pounded the table, tiles hopped. "I'm *not* miserable." The game was ruined.

"Well," she said, "maybe you're not. Maybe just

I am." She threw out her hands. "Whoever *I* am. I'm not even sure anymore. You keep trying to make me into somebody else. Into a Cricket Dupree. Sometimes I think, before you do anything or say anything to me, you check with Richie Bell first. Or you look it up in some handbook about how to have a girlfriend."

"That's crazy."

"Maybe it is." Another towel. This one she ripped into strips and let the strips float down to the basket. "I don't know. Somehow we're doing things to each other. Changing each other. I don't feel I'm who I used to be, and neither are you. And I don't *want* that. Because I liked who we used to be." She came to the table. "Want to know something sad? You're not going to believe this. You knew me better last year than you do right now."

"That *is* crazy."

She leaned over the board. "Jason, you —" her lip was quivering, but instead of backing off, she leaned in even closer — "you never even asked me how I did at the auditions." Her eyes sparkled.

"What auditions?"

She straightened up. "See? For District Band. At Great Valley."

"Oh yeah. Didn't I ask you? Hey, sure I did. I remember. Didn't I?"

She wagged her head. "No. Jason, you never never did. You weren't interested. All you did was holler at me because I was late for the dance. Did you ever ask me to play 'Trombone Troubadour' for you? Do you really believe for one instant that if you ever wrote a song, I wouldn't ask to hear it? Or if you painted a picture I wouldn't ask to see it?"

"You painted a *picture?*"

"Oh —" She headed for the paper towels.

I wanted to ask how she did at the audition. I wanted to tell her to get her trombone and play the song right then, there, in the kitchen. But it was too late. It was too late for a lot of things. But there was one thing, something I had been thinking about, asking myself about, saving. This wasn't the time or place I had in mind, but . . .

I looked deep into her eyes. "Marceline . . . I love you."

She just gaped at me for a while. Her expression started to change, but into what I never found out, because just then her mother came in.

"Hey, you two, I hope —" she stopped when her eyes landed on us, on the scrambled board; she opened the refrigerator — "that game isn't going to last all night. Marceline needs her beauty rest." She closed the fridge without taking anything out. She looked at the basket, at the paper towels overflowing onto the floor, but she didn't say anything. She left.

A minute later I was out of the house and on my way home, after Marceline said some stuff about her mother being right and there being homework left to do. She kept blinking a lot and looking every place but at me. She didn't stand outside the door, waiting until I started off on my bike, like she usually did; the door shut behind me before I hit the bottom step. There was something in my coat pocket. The ankle chain.

I pedaled home in a daze. I couldn't believe it had happened. I couldn't believe it had happened so fast. I couldn't believe it had ended where it did, me saying "I love you." I mean, things don't end when you say "I love you." They begin.

Don't they?

Spaces

She gave me a note the next day. Said she didn't mean it had to be forever. Just give it a try. See how well we get along on our own.

I waited three days and called. I said I gave it a try, and I thought it was time to get back together. She said it was too soon. We had to give it a better try.

"Valentine's coming," I said.

"I know," she said.

I bought a heart-shaped box of candy, plus a two-dollar card that unfolded as long as my wingspan. The day came. I passed her in the halls. Four times. She smiled and said hi, but she didn't stop or slow down or reach out to give me anything. I searched every inch of my locker. I held each of my books by its spine and shook it to see if anything fell out. I rushed home to check the mail. Nothing. I extended Valentine's Day till February fifteenth. Then the sixteenth. Nothing. I threw the card in the basket. Five minutes later I pulled it out and mailed it to her. I put the heart-shaped candy box in my dresser, under a sweater.

I feel so rotten. Empty. I'm leaking. Nothing stays in me. Nothing fills me up. Not food. Not school. Not friends. Not TV. Not even sleep. I wake up in the morning, and for the first couple seconds I'm like a sack full of sand, heavy and dopey. Then I remember, and the sand comes pouring out, and I'm empty again. Before my feet even touch the floor.

My old space station is sitting in the back corner of the shelf in my closet. I take it down. It's dusty, kind of mangy. Smaller than I remember. Whatever made me once think it was so great? I plug it in. Half the little colored lights don't work, and the ones that do are dull with dust. But that space station, it was new when we were new, back in seventh grade. I dust it off and put it on my table.

I hear someone humming, and it takes me back to two summers ago, when we met each other biking in the country, when we doubled up on my bike because hers had crashed into a cow, when her blowing hair tickled my face and she was humming as we sailed back into town under the pink-tinted streetlights.

I think about *Pioneer*, the spacecraft. Two summers ago it was at the edge of the solar system, but somehow I still felt in touch with it. How much farther has it gone in two years? Is it finally out past the last particle of light from the sun, plunging into blackness forever?

I look up. The universe is mostly empty. I look up at night, and all I see are the spaces between the stars.

Man

I kept thinking about Peter fighting for Jewel. And about Cricket falling in love with Richie in his mud-covered football suit. And about Vesto, who's a bastard, but who's always got two or three girls in his car.

A message kept coming through: you're too nice. It was true. I was almost sixteen, but I wasn't mean enough, and I wasn't man enough. Guys younger than me were fighting guerrilla wars in Asia and Central America. What was I going to do about it?

To start off, I kicked Cootyhead's guinea pig. She got it for Christmas. It's one of those shaggy jobs, orange and white. From the first second I saw it, I couldn't stand it. No reason, really. Guess I'm just not a guinea-pig man. Anyway, one Saturday afternoon, when Cootyhead was off malling, I snuck into her room. She was allowed to let the animal out of its cage as long as she kept her door shut and cleaned up the mess. It was just kind of nibble-nosing around on the rug. I just stood there watching it, until I couldn't take it anymore. I had to either kick it or leave the room. So I kicked it. Not real hard. Just enough to send it tumbling under the bed. Funniest thing I ever saw. For about thirty seconds.

I went over to the martial-arts place and bought a pair of nunchucks. Cheap plastic ones, but good enough to learn with. I practiced in my room. The target was one of Timmy's teddy bears.

I thought about enrolling in some class, like tae kwon do, but instead I went to the wrestling coach at school and asked if I could join the team. He looked at me like I was crazy and said I was just a teeny bit late, there were only two weeks left in the season. Then, as I was walking away, he called me back and said maybe he could use me as a practice dummy for some of the wrestlers who were getting ready for the league championships, if I was interested.

So for two weeks, every day after school, I was a wrestler. Mostly I practiced with two eighth-graders in the eighty-five-pound weight class. My job was simple: don't let them pin me. We were about ten seconds into the first practice session when I got the shock of my life. All of a sudden I'm on my back, the kid's chest is plunked on mine, and he's burying his face somewhere down below my ear. *He's trying to kiss me!* I'm thinking. But that's not all. One of his arms is smack between my legs, crunching my gonads. With all this going on, the last thing I'm thinking about is my shoulders. The other kid, who acts as referee, thumps the mat three times. "Pin!"

The rest of the day, whenever I found myself on my back, I clamped my legs together as tight as I could. But those eighty-five-pounders, they had hands like crowbars. Each time they pried me apart. I started giving up quick so I'd get pinned and we could stand up again.

I found out it was one of the most popular wrestling holds. It's called a half nelson with a deep front crotch. No wonder they don't have coed wrestling. That night I went to the sporting-goods store and got a plastic crotch cup. There were two sizes. I was going to get the small, but then I figured, shoot, no more kid stuff, go for it. Next day, it looked like there was a squirrel inside my pants.

By the second week, I had had a couple chances to try the half-nelson-crotch hold on them, but I couldn't bring myself to do it. It seemed eerie, inside out, doing that to a guy, putting my hand there, before I ever did it to a girl. But finally, during the last match of the last day, I went for it. It wasn't so bad — the eighth-grader had a cup on too. But the best part was getting him down, nailing him to the mat. It wasn't a whole pin — after two thumps he squirmed loose — but I walked out of the locker room that day with those thumps drumming in my ears. I ran all the way home.

Next day I decided to work on hair. When I was

little I used to think that by now I'd be part gorilla, hairwise. Well, I finally did get a pretty decent turf, but on my face, chest, arms, and legs it was still strictly peach fuzz, and blond, short peach fuzz at that. Ham told me not to be so anxious to shave, because once you cut a hair it comes back darker and heavier. That was all I had to hear.

I stripped down to my underpants, got my mother's can of Gillette Foamy, shook it good, and started squirting. By the time I was done, I was a teenage marshmallow. White, soft, sudsy, snowy everywhere but my nose, eyes, hands, feet, and back. Carefully, I sat down on the toilet seat. I figured I'd wait at least five minutes, give the Foamy a good chance to soak in. I reached for my mom's purple razor, and that's when the door opened. A million times Timmy's been told not to open the bathroom door when it's shut, but he still does it, and this time, coming out of her room, behind him, looking over his shoulder, was Cootyhead. For about a year nobody moved. Three pairs of moon-size eyes. Then I kicked the door shut, and the screaming started. No time to waste. I quick wiped the Foamy off with a towel, shot into my room, threw some clothes on, and was sneaking out the back door while Timmy and Cootyhead were in the cellar pleading with my mother to come up and *see*.

At school I found another guinea pig to kick, so to speak. The Rudolph-belt kid. Up till then, I had pretty much ignored him. I wasn't ever crazy about having this goggle-eyed twerp-nerd call my name and try to slap five with me, especially when I was with some guys, but then one day the kid out-nerded even himself, and I couldn't let him slide anymore.

It was during an assembly. The whole school was sitting in the auditorium. Some science guy was up on stage sticking stuff in a foaming pot, freezing the stuff solid. Like, he sticks in a grape — bam — it's a marble. So, all of a sudden there's this kid on his feet, edging his way along the row where I'm sitting, heading for the aisle. It's the nerd. His bladder's probably ready to burst. The thing is, he's not just scooting out to the aisle and up to the bathroom. No. He's fascinated by the show. Hypnotized. He's coming down the row in a trance, real slow, sometimes even stopping just to gawk, his dumb mouth wide open, like that's where his eyeballs are. Stumbling, bumbling, gawking, gaping, tromping on people's feet, knocking into the heads of the people in the next row. A girl squeals. Heads are turning. The kid is so mesmerized he doesn't even go into his usual pep rally when he notices that he's passing in front of me. He just goes, "Hi, Jason," kind of foggily, steps on my foot, and nerds on down the row and finally pops into the aisle. And what's he do then, with the whole school sitting, watching? He stands there right in the aisle, gaping at the stage. Not until the guy puts a lid on the fuming pot does the kid turn and go up the aisle.

I was sitting with my two homeroom buddies, Finney and Dustand. Finney nudged me, smirking, his voice sexy-growly: "Hi, Jason."

I elbowed him. "Some pissant seventh-grader."

Finney winked. "I thought maybe he was one of your best pals."

"I don't even know his name."

Dustand leaned over. "Catch the belt?"

Finney and Dustand were twinkling and grinning. I joined in. No way the kid was going to get back as easy as he got out.

A couple minutes later Dustand hissed: "Rudolph's back."

The kid was in the aisle, gawking again. The guy on stage was doing stuff with lasers now. My blood pressure was rising, my foot was twitching. I wanted to charge up to the kid, grab him by the neck with both hands, lift him off the floor, shake him like a can of paint, and scream into his face: "You're a nerd! Can't you see that?"

Finally the kid starts slopping his way back down our row. But this time he runs into little, unexpected problems. Like not being able to go on because somebody has a finger hooked onto the back of the reindeer belt. Like other feet tramping on his feet. Like his shirt collar being flipped up. As he passes Dustand, Dustand wets the tip of his finger and sticks it in the kid's ear. Then Finney gooses him. Actually lifts the kid onto his tiptoes. The kid takes his eyes off the stage long enough to look behind himself, and that's when I unzip his fly. He turns around, looks down, sees what I did, zips himself back up, and does the last thing I expect — he laughs.

From that day on, Rudolph was target number one. The red balls weren't shiny noses — they were bull's-eyes. It was like a rule: If your eyes landed on the kid, you had to do something to him. All day long you'd hear, "Yo, Rudy! . . . Yo, Rudy!"

The kid was so unbelievably stupid. All he had to do to make it all stop was just cry a little once and run off and disappear with the rest of the seventh-graders — and maybetake that belt off — and he'd be off the hook. But the nerd-moron did just the opposite. He laughed when you did stuff to him. Like he figured he was a ninth-grader. If nobody happened to be noticing him, he'd come over and give you a hi-there-ol'-pal punch in the arm and stand there grinning up at you, his eyes looking like guppies behind the fishbowl glasses.

But the thing that bugged me most about him wasn't his nerdishness or his looks. It was fear. He didn't have any. He should have, but he didn't. As each day went by, I took it more and more personally. Because it wasn't only him; he was just the last in a long, long line of people who weren't afraid of me. In fact, I couldn't think of anybody (except Timmy at certain times, and he didn't count) who had ever

been afraid of me. And who could blame them? Why
should they be afraid of Mr. Nice Guy? Of somebody
who was never even in a fight of his own? How did
I ever expect to become a man? How did I ever
expect to win respect? Get a girl? *Keep* a girl?

I had to hit somebody.

Fist

We were in Health. Doing lifesaving stuff. CPR. Heimlich maneuver. We did the CPR on a dummy, but for the Heimlich maneuver, we had to pair up and do it on each other. I paired up with Looie Lopezia.

First I did it to him. Then it was his turn. He stood behind me, close. I could feel his chin jutting into my shoulder. He put his arms around me, locked his hands together, nuzzled his knuckles against my gut, and rammed them up and in. Air shot out of me. His hands unlocked, but instead of falling away, they slid up my shirt and squeezed my nipples. "Hi, Marcy," he cooed.

Funny, it didn't bother me at first. In fact, I kind of liked hearing somebody say her name to me, linking us together. But then — I can't explain why exactly — it started to bother me. It stopped being a harmless little joke. I got mad. And madder as the day wore on. I thought of Peter, slugging it out for Jewel.

After school, I caught up to Looie a couple blocks away. He was lugging his suitcase-radio, blasting the neighborhood. Vesto's car wasn't in sight. I thumped him on the back. He stopped, whipped around. "Hey!"

"What was that s'posed to mean in class?"

He looked all surprised, flabbergasted. "Huh? What class?"

"Health."

"What about it?"

"You know."

He tried to change the subject. "Wha'd you just do that for?"

"Wha'd you mean by it?"

I stepped into him, chest to chest. He backed off. The blasting radio was like a roaring crowd.

"Mean by what?"

"What you did to me. When we were doing the Heimlich maneuver."

He stared, still acting all befuddled. He tried hiking the radio up under one arm, but he needed two arms to hold it that high. "What's *yer* problem?" I shoved him. He staggered back. "*Hey!*"

"I said . . . what did you mean by it?"

From the corner of my eye I saw some kids on the other side of the street. They were stopped. Watching.

"I didn't mean *nothin'!* It was a *joke!*" His voice was screechy.

"You got somethin' you wanna say about Marceline?"

"No. Why should I?"

Across the street somebody hooted, "Waste 'im!" Looie's eyes darted to the voice, back to me, wide now, the radio roaring . . .

I kept shoving him. "Huh? . . . Huh? . . . Huh? . . ." He kept lurching backward, staring. I hit him. ("Yahoo!" came the voice.) One punch. Not hard. For some reason, I knew that swinging hard had nothing to do with it. The thing was just to hit him. My closed-fist knuckles against his face. I thought it would be bone on bone, but it wasn't. My fist didn't land on his cheekbone or on his jaw, but in between, flat on the fleshy part of his cheek. It made a funny, clucky, reverse-slurp sound pop out of his mouth.

Now we just stood there, staring at each other. All afternoon I had pictured everything up to this point, but now I could see that it wasn't over yet. I wondered what to do with my fist. It seemed like there ought to be some shelf or drawer where I could stick it. Finally my fist turned into a pointing finger, jabbing at his nose: "And don't ever do it again."

That's when he started to cry. His face fell apart, his eyes flooded, he hugged his radio to his chest. "You b-basterd!" he blubbered, and he ran off. Cheers from across the street.

All the way home it was like walking on a stage. I knew people were looking at me, talking, but I pretended not to notice. Even the trees seemed to back off a little: *Don't mess with that dude.*

As long as I thought about the others watching and thinking about me, I felt pretty good. Like I took up more space than before. But if I thought about Looie, I didn't feel so good. Why did he have to start bawling like that? Why couldn't he be a man about it? Was he trying to spoil the whole thing? So I didn't think about him, and I felt better again. I wondered if I was feeling the way Peter had felt after his fight. And most of all, that night in my room, I wondered what Marceline would think when she heard. If she didn't like it at first, I'd tell her the story behind it, why I had to do it.

But by the next morning, none of it made any difference. Because I found out that she had already gone out with somebody else.

Him

I heard it from Richie, in The Stairwell.

"You saw them?" I said. My voice was raspy.

"No. Somebody in the band told Cricket."

"Who is it?"

"I don't know. He's from Marple."

"Marple?"

"Read my lips."

"You sure?"

"That's what she said."

I walked upstairs like I was mounting the gallows. I didn't think it was possible to feel any worse than I had after the night in her kitchen. That feeling was emptiness, as if somebody had scooped out my insides, like you do with a pumpkin. Now, the hatch was opened, and insides were being dumped back into me. Only thing, they weren't my insides. They felt like they had been scraped off a road somewhere.

Marple?

Marple was five miles up the pike. Another town. Another school. Did he drive? Was he older? High school? Somebody from a foreign school had gone out with Marceline. The Marceline of Jason and

Marceline. How could she do this to me? How could I possibly live to see first period? Instant intestinal flu — I ran for the bathroom.

I waited for her outside her first class. She smiled. The road scrapings inside me seemed to realize they didn't belong there; they were thumping and gnawing to get out. I concentrated hard on her face.

"What's his name?"

The smile went.

"Whose name?"

"The guy you went out with."

She looked at me for a while, like she was deciding what to answer, or whether to answer at all.

"Eric," she said.

Eric.

As soon as she spoke, I realized I had half expected her to say something like, "I forgot." But she knew the name, knew it well — I could see that — and when she said it — *zap!* — I felt gone. Erased. Replaced. Where there was Jason, now there is Eric. Eric and Marceline. Long live. Forevermore.

"I have English," she said and started walking.

I went along.

"I hear he's from Marple."

"He is." She cradled her books, stared straight ahead.

"How's that?"

"He lives there."

He. The pronoun was killing me.

"I mean . . . how'd you get to go out with a guy from there?"

She turned, glared. "What did you do, hire a detective to follow me?" I couldn't think of anything to say. The insides inside me were re-forming themselves, into something mangled and furry and still trying to drag itself across the street. She sighed, turned away. "I met him at District Band. He asked to come see me."

"He's in ninth grade?"

"Yes."

"He drive?"

"He came on the bus. My father picked him up at the bus stop."

God! Her father was in on it!

She stopped. We were at English. The way she stood, looking at the lockers, I knew she was allowing me one more question, and it had better be quick. I had a zillion. I flipped past "Do you like him?" and "Did you kiss him?" and I said, "Are you going out with him again?"

She tilted her head, her eyes changed — her eyes were seeing . . . *Eric*. She shrugged. "I don't know. Maybe." She started in.

I touched her arm. "Did you kiss him?"

She just kept going, like she didn't hear.

A slap on my back. "Hey, Herk! Hear you bopped somebody yesterday."

Rudy. Grinning. I tried to get away from him. I couldn't. He kept after me, closing in, grabbing my sleeve, jabbering, pestering, clinging. To get rid of him, I rocked my arm behind me; when I brought it back, he wasn't hanging on it anymore. I could hear him behind me, going down in a flap and flutter of flying books. I was going to turn around, but I stopped myself.

At home, I threw away the heart-shaped box of candy.

Watch

Marceline's street dead-ends at a little park. Grass, trees, a sliding board, two seesaws, and a tennis court. Marceline lives two houses from the end. So, if you stand behind one of the trees at the edge of the park, you can see her house pretty good.

As soon as it got dark Saturday, that's where I was. I hoped I was wrong. I hoped she was in her room. Alone. But I had to know. I had to see. There was no place else in the world I could possibly be.

A couple hours went by. Nothing. Windows: yellow rectangles downstairs, dark upstairs. Parents' car in the driveway. I was tempted to sneak up and peek through a dining-room window. Then the light over the front steps went on, and a second later someone — alone, man, her father — came out, buttoning his jacket. He got into the car, backed down the driveway, took off. Sometimes, if Marceline and I were at the mall, Mr. McAllister would come and pick us up. My heart was starting to bongo. My hands were damp and spongy, like the ground I stood on.

It turned out to be the fourth pair of headlights

that came down the street. All the others veered
into driveways up the way. But this pair kept coming, straight at me, and didn't turn in till two houses
from the end. A door opened, light in the car, three
shadow figures. They got out, the doors slammed
shut, the car light went out. They moved toward
the step light. He was taller than her. I strained to
hear. Nothing. They stood there while her father
unlocked the front door. I couldn't believe he was
being so cooperative. They didn't look like they were
talking. They just looked like two separate figures
somebody had left on the doorstep. The door opened.
Closed. They were in.

Pioneer could have sailed out past Pluto, past Alpha
Centauri, the nearest star, out of the Milky Way
and halfway on to the next galaxy, and it all would
have taken a minute compared to how long I had to
wait, watching that closed door, those yellow rectangles.

The door opened. They were out. On the step.
Under the light. Stopped. Facing each other. No
father in sight. Then, a small movement, the space
between them was gone. *Kissing.*

I gave them a fair enough time, but they wouldn't
stop. I couldn't stand it. I either had to stop them
or turn and run, and I couldn't turn and run. But
how to stop them? . . . How? . . .

Yell. Start yelling like hell. Nobody's gonna keep
doing anything with somebody being murdered or
raped in the park. Screech your voice. Like you're
somebody else.

So I started yelling, like I figured some victim would: "*Aaaaaaahhhhhhh-eeeeeeeeeyaaaahhhgg*." They didn't move. Still no space between them. "*Yyaaaaaaaaaaaaaaaaaa - ghhaaaaaaaaaaaaaaaaaa - ggghhhaaaaaaaaaaaaaaaaaaaaaaaaaaaaa - helllllllllpp - helllllllllllllllllllllllllllp!*" I screamed my lungs to shreds, and somewhere in there I stopped pretending I was somebody else, and I became me.

Light shone between them. The door opened. Lights plinked on up the block. Dark figures moved down driveways. One was running. I bolted for my bike. As I grabbed it, I discovered something in my hand: a big slab of bark. I wondered how it got there. I threw it away, climbed aboard, and took off as feet thumped down the sidewalks beyond the trees. When I got out of the park and circled around to go home, I saw two flashing cop cars hanging turns into her street.

Love

The first couple days of baseball, we had practice in the gym. Calisthenics, throwing, laps. Then we went outside. The infield was rutted and beachy. Onion grass stuck up like whiskers all over the outfield.

This was supposed to be my big year. My goals were to hit .350 and go the whole season without an error at shortstop. Good luck. In the first infield practice, ground balls hit me in the kneecap, the stomach, and the forehead. Everyplace but my glove.

"Spring fever?" the manager called.

Spring shit, I thought.

Across the way, in her sweats, hair bobbing, Marceline jogged around the cinder track. This year she would be the best miler on the team.

One day, as I was passing 7-Eleven on my way home from practice, I heard my name, like singing: "Jaaay-son."

It was Heather Newsome. With two other girls. All drinking Slurpees. While the other girls giggled into their straws, Heather came across the parking lot, swinging her hips like she was practicing the hula.

"Hi, Jason." Her eyes were wide, fluttery.

"Hi."

"Did you have detention? Were you a bad boy?"

"Baseball practice."

Her mouth made an oval. "Ooooo." Her lips and the tip of her tongue were cherry-colored. "Did you hit a home run?"

"Not exactly."

She puckered her lips around the red-and-white-striped straw, but I could tell she wasn't drawing any Slurpee up. Her eyes were doing the drinking, and it was me that was being sucked in. A minute later we were back behind the Dumpster.

I'd just closed my eyes when something cherryish came into my mouth. Her tongue. It didn't do it like mine used to to Marceline. It jumped right in. All business. Last time my mouth was so open I was in a dentist's chair. And fast. It took her five seconds to mop every one of my teeth. Upper, lower, inside, outside. Like a piano player thumbing down a keyboard. Suddenly she went "Ouch!" and pulled away.

"What's the matter?"

"Ny tongue." She had her tongue all the way out; it looked like half a twin cherry Popsicle. Her eyeballs were scrunching down along her nose, trying to see. Her fingertip touched the tip of her tongue. "Cayity. Shark."

"*Huh?*"

The tongue went back in. "Cavity. You have a cavity back there. It's sharp. It hurt me." Out came the tongue again. "Eeding?"

I looked. "I don't think so. It's hard to tell. It's already all red from your Slurpee."

With my own tongue I started feeling around for the cavity. I found it on the inside lower right, between two molars.

I figured that would be that, but it wasn't. She plunged right back in — up and down my gums, my cheeks, halfway down my throat. I kept shifting my tongue around to try to stay out of her way.

She started making noises. Then we stopped kissing and started hugging, and the noises turned to words. "Oh, Jason. Jason. Jason."

"What?" I said.

But that was all she had to say. "Jason. Jason. Jason." Her face was buried in my neck. I felt like I was being eaten alive. "Jason. Jason. Jason." A roach crawled out of the Dumpster. I pulled us back a step. "Jason. Jason." She was breathing like she was on the last lap of a mile race. "Jason." Squirming, like she had to go to the bathroom. "Jason." Then she switched to the other side of my neck. Then — open wide — back to France.

As soon as I got home I looked in the mirror. There they were — a pair of Class A hickeys. Real beauts. At dinner Ham said, "Timmy, he's one of the aliens now. Whatever you do, do *not* let him near your neck." But Timmy wouldn't back off till

I let him touch them. Cootyhead gagged. My mother just glared.

Next morning a breeze hit me as I opened the door. I flinched. No need — the breeze was warm. It had rained overnight, and the worms were out. Spring! And just like that, I knew this spring — the only ninth-grade spring I would ever have — wasn't going to be a waste after all.

I knew she would be waiting at 7-Eleven after practice, and she was. This time my tongue went one-on-one with hers. "Oh, Jason, oh." And when I clamped down on her neck ("Oh"), there was no pulling back ("Oh!"), not the slightest flinch, just "Ouuuuu."

I felt a hand on my butt. It slipped into my back pocket. Squeezed.

"Jason, I love you."

"Yeah," I said.

"Oh, I do. I really do."

"Yeah."

Now the other side of my butt. Into the pocket. Squeeze.

"You love me, don't you?"

"Huh?"

"Don't you love me?"

"Uh-huh."

"Are you sure?"

"Uh-huh."

"Positive?"

Squeeze. Squirm.

"Absolutely."

A minute later she asked me to go to the prom with her. When I said sure, she went into a frenzy of squealing, squeezing, and squirming.

What a feeling, to make someone that happy. *She's going apeshit over you.* Everything I did was okay with Heather. As far as she was concerned, I was perfect. I couldn't have made her mad if I tried. It was all so easy. Automatic. Why had things been so much harder with Marceline?

By the third day, Heather was talking about what color gown to wear, where to get it, what I would look like, should I wear a white dinner jacket or powder blue. "Ouuuuu," she squealed. "It's gonna feel like we're married!" Her eyes looked up to mine. They were sparkling. When she sent me a note, she signed it, "Love Forever, Heather (Herkimer)."

I loved it. At last I was in the fast lane. With everybody else. Hickeys. Making out in hallways. Even in a classroom once. The Bushes. Love letters. Ankle chain. (She had it on five seconds after I gave it to her.) The whole deal. Sometimes when we were making out, I would start out thinking only of Heather; but then I would think of Marceline; and *then* of Marceline and Eric; and then I'd go back to strictly Heather. We doubled with Richie and Cricket. Heather and Cricket got along great.

After the first baseball game, Heather was waiting by the stands. I was covered with mud from two headfirst slides on the wet infield. We stood and looked into each other's eyes. With her fingernail she dug a thin trench down the caked mud on my shirt. I told her I'd meet her as soon as I went to the locker room and changed. "No" — she sparkled — "don't change."

. . . a ride you wouldn't be-*lieve*.

So, I guess I had a right to be surprised — to be pretty damn shell-shocked, actually — when I turned a corner in school one day and practically bumped into Heather swapping spit with Hughie Muntz alongside the trophy case.

Eyes

When I saw them, I didn't say anything. I just froze for a minute, then took off. They never saw me.

I didn't need a fortune-teller. She wouldn't be waiting by the Dumpster anymore. Or by the stands. There would be no prom, not for us, anyway. No need to talk to her, call, write, beg.

It was eleven days since she had said she loved me. Loved for eleven days.

The next eleven or more I spent in a coma. Every time I swung at a pitched ball, it dipped under my bat. When I tried to catch a grounder, it slithered under my glove or attacked my chest. Heather cruised by in the hallways, clinging to Hughie, laughing, wearing my ankle chain. Then she was cruising and clinging and laughing with Alan Borg, and wearing Hughie's chain on the other ankle. Good thing she only had two legs.

What was going on? Nothing figured. This was supposed to be the best part of the best year of all. Everybody was excited about the prom. And about graduation. In less than two months — gone from here forever.

But me, I felt like I was already gone. Like I was drifting through this place where I had once gone to school; but nobody seemed to notice, and I couldn't figure it out, because I was too dumb to realize I wasn't even real anymore. I was just a ghost. A myth. Not even a memory.

Then, one day, once again, someone looked into my eyes and held me close.

It happened in the cafeteria. I was drifting through, carrying my tray, looking for the guys. I heard Finney: "Yo, Rudy! Rudy!"

Ever since I'd sent him flying in the hall that day, Rudy had been careful not to come anywhere near me. What he didn't know was that it didn't make any difference anymore. I would have just ignored him. But the others, they still cared. Every day was open season on Rudolph.

I probably wouldn't have even looked if I'd had much choice, but it was happening one row of tables over from where I was walking. It was Finney and Dustand and some others, but mostly Finney. He was the one standing. He had his back to me, practically obliterating the runt from my view. As I moved on down the aisle, I got a better look. The runt had chicken nuggets, and Finney was taking them one by one and popping them into his own mouth. The kid couldn't have gotten away if he wanted, because with his free hand Finney had hold of the kid's tray.

But of course, the stupid, moronic seventh-grader wasn't trying to get away. As usual, he was yukking it up with everybody else, getting a big charge out of all the upper-class attention. At the same time, you could see his eyes darting to his plate and see that he was getting a little worried, because it was finally sinking into his amoeba brain that — golly gee! — maybe Finney wasn't gonna stop till he ate every last little nugget. And so the runt plucks a nugget off the plate and pops it into his mouth.

"Hey, Rude!" Finney bellows like a goosed cow. "That's my nugget!" And he steps alongside the nerd and whomps him good on the back.

The kid's eyes bulged. I know this couldn't really happen, but it *looked* like they bulged out so far that they knocked his glasses clear off his face. Anyway, the glasses did topple off, onto the tray, and the stupid kid is standing there all bug-eyed and reindeer-belted, like he's going to eat the glasses for lunch. It was a comical sight, even I had to admit that. Everyone else was roaring. Watching the moron gaping at Finney, I thought: Finally, finally, you idiot, you're afraid. Now maybe you'll crawl back into your hole with the rest of the runts.

I don't know what made me start to move his way. There finally was fear in his eyes all right, but it was wrong somehow — too much. Too much for Finney, even for what had just happened. Then I was hurrying, plowing through the roaring laughter —

my lunch stuff sliding, toppling, crashing to the floor with my tray — plowing past Finney, sending him sailing, racing for the bulging eyes and the Slurpee-red face and the blueberry lips. I swung behind him, reached around, and locked my hands together just under his rib cage, just like in Health, and I rammed my fists as hard and fast as I could, in and up, aiming for the diaphragm. Nothing. Again: in and up. *Push!* Out it came. With a sound like a popped light bulb, the nugget shot out of his mouth and hit Finney, who was on the floor rubbing his head, square between the eyes.

That's when the kid finally decided to let go of his tray. It clattered to the floor along with his glasses. Then he was deadweight, sagging down through my arms, snagging buttons on my shirt. He sank to the floor, clutching his throat, heaving and hacking, all curled up.

I picked up his glasses. Other than that, nobody moved. After a while he got stiller, quiet. He was taking long, deep breaths. When he finally looked up, he squinted at all the faces gawking down at him. I handed him his glasses. He put them on. He looked all around, at the faces. His cheeks were still pink, and wet. Then his eyes fixed on me. He started to push himself up from the floor. He was weak and he could barely make it, but he kept his eyes on me every inch of the way up. Then he was standing in front of me, and tears were gleaming behind the glasses. He sobbed out something, but it didn't make sense. He tried again. "Thanks." It looked like he wanted to say more, but nothing else came out. Then he gave me a goofy smile, and then he was hugging me. I could feel him sobbing against me. Nobody made a move, not a sound. I felt funny. I wished he would let go. My arms were just dangling there. I didn't know what else to do with them, and he wasn't letting go, so I put them around him. "It's okay, kid," I whispered.

When I looked up, into the sea of faces, I saw, way in the back, another pair of eyes, another smile. Marceline's.

Be

"You get the feeling this isn't for us? It's all for them?"

"Yeah, I do."

"They're playing with us. We're dolls."

"Ken and Barbie."

"Hi, Ken."

"Hi, Barbie."

We were whispering through smiling teeth as we faced a flash camera for the sixth time that night. First at Marceline's house, then Peter's, then Jewel's, then Calvin's, then Renee's (Calvin's date; he met her at the Mutter Medical Museum — they were both looking at the liver of a beer-fed goose), and now mine, which was where Ham and I had started out from over an hour before.

"Mom," I said, "it would be nice if we got there in time for the last dance, y'know."

"Okay," my mother chirped, peeking one-eyed into the camera, "this is it . . . last one . . . smile, all . . ."

"Your finger is in front of the lens again, dear," said Ham.

Her finger swung up — "O-*kay*-ay." Behind her

Timmy and Cootyhead were pulling their mouths into revolting shapes when the blue cube became an exploding nova that atomized the living room; then, just as suddenly, it was a blue cube again, and the wrenched mouths didn't have to be looked at anymore.

The car didn't seem like ours. It seemed like a limo. Marceline and I sat up front with Ham. Backing out of the driveway, he made a couple rotten jokes; then he shut up the rest of the way. None of us said much. Mostly we looked out the windows while the girls' gowns shushed at each other. These were the same streets I walked along to school every day, the same curbs and corners I had taken on my bike for years, but it all seemed different now. Special. Dreamy. Like everything — every word, every movement, every stop sign, every tree — wore its own cummerbund or corsage. Along the way, girls were stuffing their gauzy green and pink and lavender gowns into back seats while gentlemen that used to be guys I knew stood by. A couple times I saw flashes behind picture windows.

More cameras and families ambushed us at the school, flanking the walk that led up to the front door (the only time we ever got to walk through it.) People called out our names, pleaded with us to look this way, that way. All the mothers' faces looked so happy, beaming. It seemed like there should be an altar instead of a front door. We were stars. Just for getting dressed up. I kept glancing down to make sure my fly was up. Marceline had her hand hooked inside my right arm, so I kept that arm bent, like in a sling. It felt awkward, but good.

As soon as we got inside, Marceline started steering me down the hall, away from the gym. "See you inside," called Jewel, as if she already knew what was going on.

"Where're we going?" I said.

"Oh, just outside. Just for a minute or two. I wanted to get away from everybody."

I tried to hear music from the gym, but I couldn't.

We went out a side door, by the parking lot, and started walking toward the back. She kept hold of my arm. We just walked for a while, real slow, not talking.

Then: "Jason."

"Marceline."

We looked at each other and grinned.

"You know, we hardly ever say anything about that time when we weren't . . . together."

It was true. I didn't know about her, but it wasn't because I didn't have a ton of questions. I did. But I kept stopping short of asking them. I think I was afraid of breaking the spell.

"I know," I said.

She looked at me, stared, and her eyes started to twinkle and her lips got grinnier and grinnier. She clutched my arm with both hands. "That *was* you screaming bloody murder in the park that night, wasn't it?"

I didn't say anything, not a word, but she knew instantly. She yanked on my arm, knocked her forehead into my shoulder a couple times, then staggered away from me shaking with laughter. It took her five minutes to calm down. When she came back to me, her face was red and teary. "Oh God . . . oh . . . oh," she sniffled. "Do you have a hankie?" I had one, clean for once. She dabbed at her face. Under the laugh-tears, her freckles were darker. "Were you jealous?"

I didn't want to answer. "What do you think?"

"I think you were." She waited for me to say something, but I didn't. "I know I was."

"You were?"

"Yeah. I was."

"Of Heather?"

"Uh-huh."

"Did you play Scrabble with him?"

"No. I couldn't. We played Monopoly."

"Ugh."

"Double ugh."

Crunchy under our feet. We were on the cinder track. I hadn't even realized it. We walked in silence for a while, just the crunch of the cinders and hushing of her gown against me.

"Remember the race?" I said.

The last time we had been on the track together

was seventh grade, on the track team, running the mile, each of us straining not to be the one that came in last. We almost died. Both collapsed. Somebody had to tell me afterward that I had finished ahead of her.

She nodded, smiled. We remembered.

"Marceline?"

"Yes?"

"I like it the way it is now."

She nudged closer to me. "Me too."

We were walking down the home stretch, where we had battled each other toward the finish line two springs before.

"Marceline?"

"Hm?"

"Do you think . . ."

I stopped, looked at her. There was so much I wanted to know. About the future. Like, to start with, did we *have* a future? But she was shaking her head, smiling faintly.

"Let's not think. Let's just be. You be you, and I'll be me . . . Okay?"

We came to the finish line. Which in the mile run is also the starting line. We stopped. Right on it. Kissed.

"Okay," I said.

It was almost dark. We couldn't get back in the side door, so we had to go back in the front. The spectators were gone.

At first the sounds seemed like flute notes blown

from another world. With each corner we turned, the notes stretched out, until they touched each other, and then, as we cornered the cafeteria, they became music.

Marceline stopped. "Jason, before we go in, there's something I have to tell you." Her face was serious, hurt.

The Night of the Quark swept over me. "What is it?"

"There's one thing that hasn't changed, and isn't going to change. I hate to tell you."

"*What?*"

That's when I noticed her eyes, and the sly grin broke through. "No hickeys!"

We tried kissing, but it didn't work, we were laughing so hard. Then we turned the last corner, and we were there.